McGee & Me!

Take Me Out of the Ball Game: Three Books in One

Look for other exciting McGee and Me! products from Tyndale House Publishers!

McGee and Me! Videos
#1 The Big Lie
#2 A Star in the Breaking
#3 The Not-So-Great Escape
#4 Skate Expectations
#5 Twister & Shout
#6 Back to the Drawing Board
#7 Do the Bright Thing
#8 Take Me Out of the Ball Game
#9 'Twas the Night before Christmas

Coming Spring 2000
#10 In the Nick of Time
#11 The Blunder Years
#12 Beauty in the Least

McGee and Me! New Media Kids Bible CD-Rom

McGee and Me! Sticky Situations Game
You can find Tyndale products at fine bookstores everywhere. If you are unable to find any of these products at your local bookstore, you may write for ordering information to:

Tyndale House Publishers, Inc.
Order Services
P.O. Box 80
Wheaton, IL 60189

Focus on the Family® presents

Take Me
Out of the Ball
Game

Beauty in the Least
The Blunder Years

Tyndale House Publishers, Inc.

WHEATON, ILLINOIS

Visit our exciting Web site at www.tyndale.com

McGee & Me! *Take Me Out of the Ball Game: Three Books in One*

Bill Myers is represented by the literary agency of Alive Communications, Inc., 1465 Kelly Johnson Blvd., Suite 320, Colorado Springs, CO 80920.

ISBN 0-8423-3666-4

Printed in the United States of America

07   06   05   04   03   02   01   00
7   6   5   4   3   2

CONTENTS

Take Me Out of the Ball Game

by Bill Myers

Don't look to men for help; their greatest leaders fail. . . . But happy is the man who has the God of Jacob as his helper, whose hope is in the Lord his God. (Psalm 146:3, 5, *The Living Bible*)

ONE
Time Tracker to the Rescue

Although worn and weary, my wonderfully worthy body stumbled into the nearest 7-Eleven. What a day! All I needed now was to drown my sorrows in a couple dozen cans of Diet Pepsi, three bags of Chee•tos, eight packages of Twinkies, and a dozen or so Gooey Chewy bars. That should hold me over during the twenty-minute drive home to dinner.

But, back to my day. As the most experienced (and, of course, the best dressed) time tracker this side of the twenty-third century, I had been chosen to time-port back to the 1800s. It seems some writer-type guy by the name of Hands Christian Anderson was having problems with one of his kids' stories. It was about this little girl fish falling in love with a sailor.

"Dis is one lu-lu of an ideea," he kept saying. "And I sink I'll call et 'De Liddle Sardine.'"

"No, Handsy-boy, sweetheart, babe," I argued in my best Hollywoodeese. "You got to think splashier, more sensational. You got to think big, big, BIG!"

"Big?" he asked. Then after a moment his eyes lit up. "Yumppen yimminie, I got et! I can see et now. I'll call et 'De Liddle Whale!'"

I let out a sigh and murmured, "Mermaid . . . What about 'The Little Mermaid'?"

He shook his head fiercely. "Nah . . . dat vill never sell."

We argued all day and night. Back and forth. Forth and back. Talk about stubborn . . . if this guy was any more bull-headed he'd be sprouting horns and chasing red capes.

Finally he gave in. But only after I promised to bring a Big Mac and a side of fries the next time I dropped by his century.

Yes-siree-bob, another dramatic job dynamically done. As usual, I was mesmerized by my incredible ingenuity while I reached over to press the portable Time Transporter strapped to my wrist. But just as my finger reached the button, my keen eye spotted another book.

"What's this, Handsy?" I asked.

"Dat's my next masterpiece," he said, beaming. "Et's all about dis princess and all dees mattresses she has to sleep on and—"

"What's it called?" I interrupted, somehow fearing the worst.

"I call et—" he gave a big proud grin—"I call et 'De Princess and de Watermelon'!"

I released the button on my wrist and let out a sigh. It was going to be another long day.

But all of that was behind me now. Now I was in my favorite 7-Eleven about to eat my weight in chips, candies, and cakes. It was a junk-food junkie's dream.

But wait a minute, something was wrong! That smell. Instead of the wondrous aroma of deep-fried and choles-terol-coated goodies, I smelled, oh no! Could it be . . . but, yes, yes . . . horror of horrors . . . it was . . .

HEALTH FOOD!

I spun around and let out a gasp. Behind me were rows and

4

rows of fresh fruits and vegetables. Everywhere I looked there was food that was actually healthy to eat. Suddenly my dream was turning into a nightmare.

I could feel my body begin to tremble. Such healthy munchies were more than I could manage. "Where . . . where's the junk food?" I nervously stuttered to the clerk.

"Junk food?" he asked blankly.

"Yeah, you know, like candy, chips, and all those other wonderful artery pluggers?"

"Well, the celery chips are in aisle three, and the carrot candy is over in aisle—"

"NO, NO, NO!" I shouted. My whole body was beginning to shake. I was going through junk food withdrawal. If I didn't consume a good hit of empty calories in the next few minutes, it was going to get ugly. My wonderful layers of fat would start to dissolve, and my chances of a stroke (or at least a good bypass operation) would disappear forever. "Please," I begged. "I need something sweet and crunchy!!"

"Well, we have some raisins and granola bars over in—"

"NO! YOU NINNY!!" I shouted, grabbing his collar and pulling him directly into my face. "I'm talking GREASE!! Sensational, salt-saturated, sugar-sprinkled, deep-fried GREASE!!"

But the look on his face said he'd never heard the word. Somehow the phrase "junk food" had not made it into his vocabulary. And then it hit me . . .

Dr. Dastardly!!

Of course. My arch rival, the twisted Time Traveler who treks back in time to foul up history. The boisterous bad guy who was responsible for you having to go to school five days a week with two days off. (It's true. The guy who originally invented school wanted it the other way around—two days of school and five days off.) The vile villain responsible for creating that secret ingredient in milk shakes that gives you headaches when you drink them too fast. And, worst of all worsts, the fiendish fiend responsible for those ridiculous prices they charge at theaters for soda pop and candy.

He had struck again. But this was by far his worst blow to humanity. Dr. Dastardly had gone back in time and somehow uninvented junk food!

Quicker than you can say polyunsaturated I reached into my coat and pulled out my time chart. A-ha, just as I figured. Dastardly's homing device showed him back in 1914. I locked onto his quadrants, pressed my Transporter button and—

Snap-crackle-zit!

I was in 1914.

Sure enough, there in front of me was Doc Dastardly. And he was standing beside the world-renowned food inventor— the founding father of junk food—the one and only Professor Potat O. Chip. True to form, the honorable gourmet was hovering over his vat of boiling oil. But he was not trying to make potato chips. Somehow Dastardly had convinced him to give up on potatoes and start working with cauliflower!

"Dastardly," I called, my voice shaky and my stomach already churning over the thought of cauliflower chips.

He spun around and looked at me. "I knew you'd come," he sneered, and I could tell he'd gotten an A in the sleazy sneer class at Bad Guy School. "It's been a long time."

"Ever since Book #4," I agreed. But this wasn't a time for nostalgia. I had a job to do, and as usual I'd do it well. "So are you going to come quietly," I asked, "or do I have to—" But I never finished the sentence.

Suddenly he raised a fresh raw carrot to his lips. Before I

could scream in protest he chomped down and took a bite out of the hopelessly healthful vegetable.

The pain was fierce, but I carried on. With an uproarious roar I raced toward the vile villainous villain, but he threw everything he had at me. First he ate pitted prunes . . . then fresh turnip greens. . . . Next came the asparagus and raw broccoli.

I began to stagger. The pain was too much. Everything began to spin. I was about to pass out.

Seeing I was on the ropes, he quickly downed three cans of V8 juice in the hopes of finishing me off. He nearly succeeded. And yet, somehow, remarkably (and, of course, quite heroically) I continued to stagger forward.

Finally he reached into his Spandex muscle shirt and pulled out his secret weapon. It was a bag of vitamins! I gasped in horror. "No!" I begged. "Not that. Please, please, anything but—"

He let out another sinister laugh and then started pelting them at me. A B-12 there, a vitamin C here, and then there was the dreaded iron supplement. The pain was just too much. I fell to my knees in agony as the horrendous pills of pure health pelted my pudgy body. And yet miraculously I managed to hang on. (I had to—I have eight more chapters to go in this book.)

Then I saw it. A remnant from the good old days. A reminder of when I and the rest of the world could stuff ourselves to oblivious obesity. It was a crumb—from a corn chip. It was stuck to my argyle sock. I reached for it with trembling hands of thankfulness.

Now it was the Doc's turn to gasp in horror.

Quicker than you can say Frito-Lay, I rose to my feet. A grin of victory spread across my perfect pearlies as I began to approach the quivering mass of cowardice.

"No!" he screamed. "Get away—get away with that!"

I continued to head for him, holding the corn-chip crumb before me. Of course, I desperately wanted to eat the delightful delicacy. But I was made of firmer (or is it flabbier?) stuff than that.

Then it happened. I was less than four feet away when I stepped on a pile of rutabagas. My nimble feet flew out from under me and sent me crashing to the floor.

Dastardly jumped up and leaped on me. Now we were in each other's grip, locked in mortal hand-to-hand combat. But as fiercely as my foe fought, it was his breath that nearly killed me. (The man had obviously slipped some parsley into his mouth when I wasn't looking, and now everything smelled fresh and wholesome.)

Then, just when I was about to do what every superhero and all-around good-looking good guy does—destroy evil (or at least mess up its hair a lot)—the dastardly Doc hit his Time Transporter and—snap-crackle-zit!—he disappeared into another century.

Rats! I hate it when he does that.

Who knew what sinister schemes his slimy soul was scheming—what terrifying trauma he would be touting? But that was OK. Once again good had triumphed over evil. Once again your handsomely heroic hero beat your villainous villain. And once again the world would be a sweeter, crunchier, and slightly saltier place to live in.

"Yo, Professor," I said, tossing a spud across the room into Mr. Potato Head's vat of boiling oil. "Have a few empty carbos on me. I'd love to stick around, but I have a little shopping to do. . . ." With that I reached for my Time Transporter and—

Snap-crackle-zit!

Pig-out city, here I come. . . .

TWO
"Take Me Out to the Ball Game . . ."

Things were not going well for little Roger Goreman. Not well at all. For years the little guy had dreamed of being a film director. That's all he wanted. Just to take his folks' video camera and make movies. Shucks, if it made his dad happy he wouldn't even mind making movies of sporting events.

What he did mind was being made to *play* in those events. What he minded even more was that he was standing at home plate with two strikes against him. And what he minded most of all was that it was the last inning of the game, his team was one run behind, and everyone was depending on him to knock the tying run home and score so they could win the Eastfield City Championship.

Nope. It was not a good day for little Roger Goreman.

Come to think of it, it wasn't such a hot day for Mr. Martin, Nicholas's dad, either. This was Mr. Martin's second year coaching. For two years now he had been working with the kids—teaching them to field, to hit, to run bases. And now it all came down to little Roger Goreman, the weakest link in the Eastfield Braves Little League team.

"C'mon, Roger babe, you can do it. Concentrate now

. . . concentrate. Bear down, man, he's all yours, babe, a piece of cake, you can do it."

At least that's what Dad was saying on the outside. On the inside he was saying: "We're sunk, we're dead, we're history."

Roger stepped closer to the plate. He took a few practice swings and waited. He tried to swallow, but there was nothing left to swallow. Apparently all the moisture in his body had migrated to the palms of his hands.

The grandstands were roaring with anxious moms and dads.

The dugouts were filled with screaming kids.

Everyone figured it was all up to Roger. Well, almost everyone . . .

It seems Nicholas and Louis didn't even bother to get to their feet. Oh sure, they wanted to win like everyone else on the team. But they knew there was another card left to play. They knew there was a secret weapon everyone had temporarily forgotten about.

The pitcher took his windup. He checked the runner on second. And then after a pause, he let the ball fly. At first it looked like a hot sizzler right across the plate. At first it looked like the Eastfield Braves were on their way to losing another championship.

But then, miracle of miracles, the ball began to rise. Then it began to curve to the outside. Could it be? Yes! Wonder of wonders, it looked like it was going to be ball four! It looked like Roger was going to be able to walk. It looked like things were finally going right after all.

The only problem was that nobody bothered to tell Roger what it looked like. Knowing it all depended on him, Roger didn't think about checking whether it was a strike or a ball. Instead he reared back and took a healthy swing for all he was worth.

"OH NO!" the crowd gasped.

"Strike three!" the umpire bellowed.

"It figures," Dad muttered.

But Nicholas and Louis weren't worried. That was only two outs. There was one man to go. And nobody, I mean *nobody*, could stop this man. . . .

"Bottom of the ninth, two away," the announcer's voice boomed across the speakers.

Nicholas leaned against the wall of the dugout and clasped his hands behind his head. "It's in the bag," he said to Louis with a grin.

"A walk in the park," Louis agreed, tipping his hat over his eyes.

"Next batter up for the Braves," the announcer called, "Pitcher, Thurman Miller!"

Suddenly the crowd was back on its feet shouting and clapping for joy. They had remembered what Nicholas and Louis had known all along. Now everyone was hooting and cheering in gleeful anticipation.

Well, almost everyone . . .

It seems the pitcher of the opposite team wasn't doing a lot of cheering. Neither was his coach. Come to think of it, the other eight players in the field weren't doing many handsprings, either.

All eyes turned to the Braves' dugout as Thurman Miller emerged . . . and emerged . . . and emerged some more. To call this kid "big" was like calling King Kong a slightly overfed chimp. For a thirteen-year-old, this guy was gigantic. We're not just talking tall, either. I mean, every-where you looked on this 5' 10" giant there was strength and power. In fact, when he flexed, even his muscles had muscles.

He grabbed a bat and strode toward the plate. The ground shook, the umpire moved back just a step, and mothers pulled their babies in a little closer for protection.

"OK, big fella, you can do it, you can do it!" Dad was shouting. "Out of the park, big guy, out of the park!"

The pitcher for the opposing team took off his cap and wiped the beads of perspiration that had suddenly appeared on his brow. He threw a glance to the score-board: 4 to 3. They were ahead by one run. He looked at the runner on second. If Thurman hit a double, this man would be the tying run. He looked back to Thurman. Of course, if Goliath there hit a homer, the big guy would score the winning run.

The pitcher took a deep breath and tried to swallow. But it was his turn for a dry mouth. It was his turn for sweaty palms.

Everyone waited.

Finally he started his windup. Then he fired the fastest fastball he had ever thrown in his life. It was beautiful—a sight to behold as it streaked toward the plate. *All right! Perfect pitch!* his mind was thinking.

The only problem was that that was also what Thurman was thinking. The big fellow leaned back and turned the perfect pitch into a perfect hit.

CRACK!

The ball sailed.

The jaws dropped.

And Thurman yawned. "What a bother," he muttered as he dropped the bat and started to run. "I go to all the trouble of hitting that ball, and now I have to run around these stupid bases."

But Thurman didn't have to run. He could take his time. I don't want to say that the ball sailed too far out of the park or that it went too high. The fact that NASA reported one of its satellites was destroyed by a round, white UFO at that exact time was probably just a coincidence.

The crowd was on its feet cheering, and Nick and Louis were high-fiving. "All right! We did it!" they shouted as Thurman rounded third and came in to home.

Everyone piled out of the dugout and raced toward the big guy. It took a little doing—and every available player on the team—but eventually they were able to hoist Thurman up on their shoulders.

"All right, Thurman!" Nick groaned as he staggered under the weight of the big kid. "Whatta hit! Whatta play!"

"What a load!" Louis gasped as he fought to hold him up.

By now everybody was on the field shouting and slapping one another on the back. "All right! Eastfield champs! We did it! . . . Nice work!"

"Great job, Thurman," Dad called as he pushed his way through the crowd to the boy. "Everybody, you were terrific!"

The kids let out another cheer.

"Listen up!" he shouted. "We're the Eastfield City Champions now!"

More shouting and cheering.

"Regional finals, here we come!" Louis yelled.

Nicholas joined in. "Then Thurman takes us right to the Little League Series!"

More cheering. Also a few groans. By the look of pain across some of the guys' faces, it definitely was time to lower Thurman back to the ground.

"Great game, son."

Louis turned around to see his mom and dad. They were a handsome couple. Like many couples their age, they were so busy with their careers that they hardly had time to be a family. Why, with Louis's mom's work as a legal secretary and his dad's job as a doctor at the clinic, they hardly had time to eat meals together, much less enjoy a Saturday ball game. But today was different. And for that Louis was very grateful.

"You made some great plays," his dad said beaming as he reached out to shake Louis's hand.

But this was no time for just a handshake. Before his dad knew it, Louis dove in for a big-time bear hug. "Thanks!" he shouted into his father's chest.

Catching Mr. Martin's eye, Louis's dad raised his camera. "Think we ought to give some of these pictures to the *Eastfield Daily News?*"

Nick's dad grinned. After all, that was the paper he worked for. But before he could answer, Louis piped up: "Nah, give *Sports Illustrated* first crack."

The men chuckled as the boys moved off. Yes sir, victory was sweet. For both kids and grown-ups.

Oh yeah, victory's sweet all right. But what about us little guys? You know, us incurably cute imaginary cartoon character types that fellas like Nicholas draw for a little spice in their life. What about us?

Oh, I'm all for baseball, don't get me wrong. In fact, in my younger days I used to pitch for the Chicago Clubs out in Wiggley Field. That is, until I threw my arm out. You know, we looked everywhere for it, but to this day we still haven't found that arm. Luckily I was able to talk Nick into drawing me another one.

Yes-siree-bob, I'm all for baseball. But I'm also all for not being forgotten. So as ol' Nicky-boy was gathering his gear, I figured it would be a good time to mesmerize his mind with some catchy catching.

"Hey, Nick!" I shouted. "Let's see the ol' knuckle-ball!"

My little buddy stopped and nervously glanced around, hoping nobody saw me. But he didn't have much to worry about. As a figment of his imagination, there wasn't much chance that I would be seen by others.

"What are you doing here?" he demanded.

"Hey, look, bright eyes," I countered. "You're the one who brought the sketch pad."

Nick threw a glance to his backpack. Sure enough, there on top, in all of its yellow-covered and spiral-ringed glory was my home sweet home.

"C'mon!" I shouted, pounding my fist into my glove, "give me your best stuff!"

Nick hesitated a minute. Obviously the poor boy didn't want to be shown up.

"C'mon," I insisted. "Let's see the ol' slider, the ol' fastball, the ol' curveball, the ol' . . ."

15

And then, rising to my challenge, he let go the mightiest pitch of all times.

But I tell you, no matter how powerful the pitch, no matter how blazing the ball, no matter how many times it bounces and almost rolls to a stop before it gets to you . . . a seven-inch cartoon character trying to catch a three-inch hardball does not make for a pretty sight.

I'll save you all the gory details about how far it bashed me into the ground. Let's just say I became the first person in history who had to reach up to touch his toes.

THREE
"Buy Me Some Peanuts and Cracker Jack. . . ."

A few minutes later most of the Braves team was piled in front of the counter of Ingrid's Incredible Ice Cream Shop.

No one's sure how going to the shop ended up being a tradition. Originally, Dad used to take team members out for pizza every time they won. But that was last year. Back in the good ol' days when, if they were lucky, the team might win one or two games. Then it got better. A lot better. And, as the team got better, Dad got cheaper.

"Great," Louis had muttered, "next year he'll probably just buy us gum balls."

At least for now it was ice cream. And everyone was chowing down. Especially Thurman.

"Don't you have any bigger dishes?" he asked as he sprinkled what must have been the 100th topping on his quadruple-decker.

"We've got a bucket in the back," Ingrid said with a grin.

Thurman didn't hear. He was concentrating on finding room for topping number 101.

Meanwhile, off in the corner, Nicholas and Louis were doing what they did best. They were bugging each other.

It wasn't the type of bugging that creeps do to noncreeps. This was the type of bugging that only best friends can do to best friends. This was the type of bugging that comes from being so comfortable around each other that you can say or be anything you want—even if you're not always as polite as you should be.

Today they were haggling over baseball cards.

"Listen," Louis said nervously. Both boys were peering over their cards at each other as intently as a couple of poker players in an old Western. But by the look on Louis's face the "game" wasn't going as well as he had hoped. Apparently Nicholas had the upper hand. "I'll, uh . . . I'll give you Guerrero, Robin Yount, and, uh . . . ," Louis hesitated a moment. Now it was getting crucial. One false move, and he could blow the whole deal. "Uh . . . Ricky Henderson!" he finished with a nervous smile. "You can't beat that!"

Nicholas grinned. You couldn't fool him. He had Louis on the ropes, and he knew it. Now it was time to go in for the kill. "You'll have to do better than that, Bucko, if you want Will Clark's *rookie* card!"

"Oh, man," Louis groaned.

Now it's true, these were just baseball cards. But to the guys it couldn't get any more tense than if they were dealing stock on Wall Street.

"Listen, Louis," Nicholas said trying to console him (after all, they were good friends). "That's a decent offer and stuff. But I'm not interested in parting with Will Clark. Not at any price. *No reason. No how. No way!*"

Suddenly Thurman's meaty paw appeared and neatly plucked the Will Clark card out of Nick's deck. "All right!" he exclaimed as he plopped down beside them. "A present for me?"

"Hey, big guy," Nicholas said without a blink, "he's all yours." He threw a glance over to Louis who was so impressed with Nick's cowardice that he accidentally broke the plastic spoon off in his mouth.

"Thanks." Thurman grinned as he nonchalantly folded and crammed the precious card into his pocket. The boys' mouths dropped open. If thoughts could be heard, their anguished cries would have shattered every window in the shop: "That's Will Clark he's demolishing!"

"Hey, how 'bout that last pitch?" Thurman laughed.

At first the guys didn't hear—either because of all the ice cream in Thurman's mouth or because they were still staring at the little lump of what used to be a baseball card stuffed in the big fellow's pocket.

In any case, Thurman didn't notice. He just kept right on eating and right on talking. "No way I'm gonna let that bozo get a fastball by me." He continued to laugh, his mouth full of strawberries, blueberries, Oreo chips, pralines, caramel sauce, chocolate sprinkles, and a dab of raspberry ripple ice cream. Not a pretty sight.

But somehow Nick was able to force a grin. "You said it!" he agreed, putting on his best I'm-going-to-pretend-I-like-this-guy-even-though-he-just-ripped-off-my-favorite-baseball-card grin. "No way. Right, Louis?"

Louis was still staring at the wadded lump in Thurman's pocket.

"Yo, Louis?" Nick repeated.

"No way . . . no how . . . ," Louis mumbled, still staring at the pocket.

"Hey!" Thurman shouted angrily.

Suddenly Louis snapped back to reality. But Thurman wasn't yelling at him. He was staring at his ice cream.

"She forgot my walnuts!" he growled.

Both boys watched with fascination as Thurman rose to his feet and lumbered back toward the counter. What few Braves there were still in line stepped aside as he approached. They'd waited this long for some ice cream, a little longer wouldn't hurt. In fact, by the look on Thurman's face, it might actually prove to be healthier to wait.

"Hey," another voice called. "Get a load of the All-Stars!"

Nicholas gave a little shudder. He immediately recognized the voice. It belonged to one of Derrick's dorks. And where his dorks were, Derrick Cryder, the all-school bad guy, was soon to follow. Maybe if Nick kept his back to him, Derrick wouldn't notice he was there. Maybe if Nick covered the side of his face with his hand. Maybe if—

"Hey, Martin!" Derrick shouted at him from across the room.

Then again, maybe not.

"What's with these outfits?" the bully jeered as he sauntered toward him. "Your Girl Scout troop on a field trip?"

"Lay off, Cryder," Nick said, trying his best to sound tough. Ever since he had beaten Derrick in the skateboard race, Nicholas knew that the guy really respected him, deep down inside—deep, *deep* down inside. The only problem was that it was so deep the guy didn't know it yet. So Nicholas would call his bluff by sounding cool and in control.

"We happen to be celebrating," he said in his most casual tone of voice. "We're the new city champs."

"You mean 'city *chumps*,'" Derrick sneered as he reached out and grabbed Nick's hat.

So much for bluffing.

"Hey, is this hat full of mush . . . like your head?" It was a stupid joke, but because Derrick Cryder made it, Derrick Cryder laughed at it. And because Derrick Cryder laughed at it, so did his dorks. That was the price of dorkhood.

"Knock it off, Derrick!" Nicholas protested. "And give me my hat." Nick tried to grab it, but his size and height were no match for the bigger kid.

"Oh, yeah," Derrick taunted. "You and whose army?" Once again his comeback wasn't all that funny. In fact, it didn't even make that much sense. But once again the dorks gave the required laugh. That is until a mammoth hand suddenly reached over and grabbed Derrick Cryder's left earlobe.

"YEOWWWWWW!!!" Derrick screamed.

All eyes followed the mammoth hand up to the mammoth arm, up to the mammoth chest of—you guessed it—Thurman Miller.

"Nice earring," Thurman grinned as he fingered the golden stud in Derrick's lobe.

"Let go, let go!" Derrick demanded. He tried to squirm, to see who dared touch his prized possession, but one twist of Thurman's hand put a stop to that in a hurry. A big hurry.

21

"OOOWWWWWWW!"

"I bet it'd hurt real bad if you lost this earring," Thurman said, thinking out loud.

Again Derrick tried to get a look, and again Thurman froze him in his tracks with another tug.

"OOOOOOOOO!" Derrick cried.

"It's real pretty, too." Thurman smiled. "My little sister has one just like it."

By now Derrick had learned his lesson. He wasn't moving a muscle.

Finally, after Thurman was sure he had made his point, he very gently and oh, so politely growled, "You wanna give back the hat now?"

"OK, OK, OK," Derrick cried as he quickly tossed the hat back to Nicholas.

At last Thurman released his ear, with just a little tweak and twist tossed in for good measure.

Quickly Derrick spun around, ready to destroy whoever had humiliated him . . . that is until he saw Thurman. Well, actually, to be more specific, until he saw Thurman's muscles. Thurman's muscles and his smile. A smile that was quickly turning to a frown.

Suddenly, for the first time in his life, Derrick Cryder knew fear.

"Beat it," Thurman said with a scowl.

And beat it Derrick did in a hurry—a big hurry, with his dorks quickly following after him.

Nick and Louis looked on with awe. Watching Thurman handle Derrick was like watching a master artist at work. But the big guy paid little attention. Instead he plopped down like nothing had happened—like traumatizing the town terror was just part of his daily routine.

An instant later Thurman's scowl returned. "One of you guys wanna get me a napkin?" he asked as he looked to the boys.

"I'll get it," Nick said as he jumped from his chair.

"Let me," Louis argued.

"I got it," Nick insisted.

Now it was a race to see who would be the first to the counter and back again with the prized napkin for their brand-new protector and all-around idol. . . .

Mom poured Dad a cup of coffee as the kids cleared the dinner dishes from the table. All the time they were eating Nick had gone on and on about Thurman Miller. He talked about him through Grandma's pork chops, sauerkraut, and potatoes. And he talked about him through little Jamie's failed attempt at dessert—strawberry Jell-O with whipped cream. The whipped cream part came out OK. But something went haywire with the Jell-O. So instead of enjoying nice jiggly strawberry Jell-O, everyone was enjoying nice slurpy strawberry soup. Of course, no one mentioned it to Jamie. After all, she was only in second grade, and they didn't want to give her some sort of anticooking complex.

"He'll probably be signed right out of high school," Nick continued as he scooped the glasses up and headed for the sink, "with a major league contract for a million dollars!"

"OK!" Sarah sighed her world-famous big sister sigh. "Enough about Thurman *Munster*, already!"

"That's Miller, not Munster," Nick corrected.

"I call 'em like I see 'em," she snipped.

"All right, you two," Dad interrupted. Like any good dad he knew when an argument was about to break out. And like any good dad he wasn't in the mood for listening to one. Still, he felt Nick had a good point about Thurman's talents. "The kid is amazing," he confessed to Mom. "No one can deny that. Nick's probably right about the pros, too. Thurman's definitely major league material."

By now Sarah was at the sink. Try as she might, she couldn't resist the temptation of banging the plates down just a little too hard on the counter, then scraping them just a little too vigorously. "Oh yes," she sighed dreamily. "And just think, the next step is *real* greatness . . . when they name a candy bar after him!"

Nicholas completely missed the sarcasm. Instead, for the first time in his life, he actually agreed with his sister. "Hey, you're right!" he exclaimed. "Like 'Miller Munchies' or . . . or 'Thurman Thingles.'"

"Thurman Thingles!" Sarah groaned in her best how-can-I-live-with-such-a-hopeless-case-for-a-little-brother voice.

But before Nick could respond, the phone rang.

"Hello?" Mom answered. "Oh, sure. Hang on." She held the phone out to Dad with a half smile. "It's for you . . . Coach."

A puzzled look crossed Dad's face as he reached for the phone. "Hello?" The puzzled look quickly turned into a depressed look. "Oh, hi, Harvey."

"Who's that, Mom?" Sarah asked.

Mom shook her head in amusement and answered, "Let's just say it isn't Publisher's Clearing House."

"What? You're kidding." Suddenly Dad's voice took on an even gloomier tone. He removed the receiver from his ear so the rest of the family could hear the snorts of laughter coming from the other end. They were so loud and obnoxious they could almost have come from Arnold the Pig instead of Harvey the whomever.

The family glanced at one another in amazement. What on earth . . . ?

"Oh, sure." Dad was back on the phone. "I can hardly wait—it'll be like old times." He rolled his eyes as more snorting came through the receiver. Then finally he brought the conversation to an end. "Right . . . see you next week." With that, he hung up and finished his sentence, "You big bag of wind."

"David . . . ," Mom admonished lightly.

"Well, of all the crummy breaks," Dad grumbled.

"Who was that?" little Jamie asked.

"Harvey Stover," Dad grumbled, "the biggest blowhard in the league. He's managing the team we're playing in the regionals."

"So?" asked Nick.

"So-o?" Dad looked at him with surprise. "You've got a short memory, Son. His team knocked us out of the play-offs last year!"

"Oh, of course!" Nick said, finally catching on. "The guy who snorts!"

"Bingo," Dad answered. Then suddenly his voice got very low and very serious. "Well, I promise you one thing.

Not this year! Things are going to be different this time around, ol' Harvey-boy!"

Mom threw a nervous glance in his direction. Dad . . . Mr. Level-Headed, Mr. Always-in-Control . . . Mr. Spiritual-Leader-of-the-Home . . . was having a problem. It didn't happen often. But, once in a while, it happened. It probably had something to do with his being human.

"No sir, buddy-boy," he muttered, growing more serious. "This year I get even. This year it's payback time." With that he grabbed his fork and jabbed it squarely into the last piece of cantaloupe. "Yes sir," he continued, "this year we've got Thurman Miller!" He plopped the cantaloupe into his mouth and chewed with relish.

Nick, who was caught up in his father's spell of victory, couldn't help breaking into a big grin.

Mom, on the other hand, was not grinning. Somehow she sensed that things were going to get a little sticky around the old homestead. Somehow she knew that some attitudes weren't entirely right. And that meant that maybe, just maybe, the Lord would be stepping in to do a little attitude adjustment. . . .

FOUR
"I Don't Care if I Ever Get Back. . . ."

The crowd gasped as I entered the arena and sauntered toward the weight-lifting platform. Up until now they had only read of my amazing strength (and incredibly manicured pinkies), but now, at last, they were able to see it. I bulged my biceps, tried my triceps, and toided my deltoids. Young women were swooning. Young men were green with envy.

And why not? After all, it was I, The Regrettable Bulk . . . world-famous wrestler and soon-to-be Weight-Lifting Champion of the World!

I glanced up to the platform. My arch rival, Nick the Hick, that towering, two-ton terror from Tennessee, was about to tout some tremendous tonnage.

A hush fell over the crowd as he reached down to the barbell. For a moment he hesitated. Obviously the kid was dreaming of all that prize money. Money that would fulfill his wildest dreams . . . cars, houses, all the CDs he could fit in his spacious, state-of-the-art rec room. Money that, if he was lucky, just might cover most of his chiropractic bills.

For months we'd been training for this one event. The Hick with all of his farm activities . . . you know, like bailing hay, chopping cotton, bench pressing tractors. And me with my excruciatingly intensive workouts of watching MTV, Nickel-

odeon, and—when I was feeling exceptionally strong—slipping in a little Mr. Rogers.

Then of course there were our diets. The Hick had his special meals of organically grown vegetables, farm-fresh fruit, and whole goat's milk. I, on the other hand, disciplined myself by eating all the junk food from chapter 1.

Now at last we were ready. With an earth-shattering cry, the Hick hoisted the barbell to his waist. The crowd ooohed. Then with a mighty shout he pushed it high over his head before leaping out of the way and letting it crash back to the platform.

The crowd was on its feet clapping and cheering wildly. Some were even throwing roses. I showed my enthusiasm by trying to stifle a yawn. Sure, he had just set a new record by pressing over two thousand pounds. But hey, what's a ton or two between such sinuous superstars as ourselves? The contest wasn't over. Not by a long shot.

Now it was my turn. Without a moment's hesitation I strutted onto the stage. Quickly I reached down and placed my hands on the long bar of the barbell, and with a mighty shout tried to lift it. It wouldn't budge. I tried again. Hey, what's the big idea—somebody bolt this to the stage or somethin'?

First the audience began to snicker. Then they began to laugh. Next they began to hoot—then boo. I glanced down at my hands. Wait a minute! This was no barbell I was trying to lift! This was one of the roses they had thrown on the stage.

I gave one last heave-ho but with no luck. So the audience decided to give the heave-ho a try, too—with me. "Get him off!" they shouted. "We want our money back!"

In its fury, the crowd began to climb onto the stage and race toward me. Now don't get me wrong. I love adoring fans as

much as the next incredible (and perfectly manicured) superstar. But these guys looked like they were after more than just
my autograph.

I turned and started to run, but they were coming at me
from all sides.

"Nicholas!" I shouted. "Nicholas get me out of here!"

"McGee!" I could hear my little buddy's voice, but I couldn't
see him.

"NICHOLAS!"

"McGee . . . McGee, snap out of it. McGEE!"

Suddenly I was back in Nick's bedroom. The arena had dissolved and so had my adoring fans. What a pity, and we were
getting to be such close friends, too.

"You were having another daydream," Nicholas said
between grunts. He was working out on his weight machine.

"More like a daymare," I said with a shudder.

Nick gave a smirk as he continued his workout. Mind you,
this wasn't just any weight machine. This was your Handy-
Dandy-Homemade-with-a-Pile-of-Encyclopedias-Tied-Together
-with-Ropes-that-Lead-to-Pulleys-in-the-Ceiling-and-Come-
Back-Down weight machine. One of our better inventions, if
I do say so myself.

Yes-siree-bob, I was back in reality, sitting at my own weight
machine, where for several minutes I had been suffering, agonizing, and worst of all, actually sweating. That's right, I'm
not ashamed to admit it. I'd actually begun to work up a dew
on my incredible, manly brow. Sweat—what an awful invention. Worse than veggie burgers or even turkey hot dogs. OK,
well, maybe not that bad, but not a lot of fun—especially when
you're a cartoon character painted with watercolors that run
when they get damp.

Anyway, Nick and I kept pulling on the weights, again and again . . . and again some more.

"Ghuuuh," I groaned as I gave another tug. "Refresh my memory. What's the point of all this?"

"Strength," Nick gasped between pulls. "If you're strong, you can't lose. Just look at Thurman. He hit that homer today because of all the power in his forearms."

"Four arms," I groaned. "No wonder I can't lift this thing. I've only got two arms!" I tried one last pull, but it was more than I could handle. Before I knew it the weights went crashing down. Unfortunately, I forgot to let go. So as the weights went crashing down, my arms went shooting up . . . stretching like a wad of Silly Putty on a hot summer day.

"See how the training helps?" Nick said with a snicker. "You're already improving your reach."

I began rolling in my arms like giant garden hoses. "Ho-ho," I sneered, "that's rich." But before I could hit him with one of my world-class, Triple-A, snappy comebacks, Dad opened the door.

"Well," he said grinning one of his famous fatherly grins. "How's the weight training coming?"

"Oh, hi, Dad," Nick answered as he glanced around to make sure I was out of sight. "I'm just taking a little break."

"Good idea." Mr. Dad nodded. "You gotta take it easy when you first get started." By now he had moved in for a closer look at our incredible, do-it-yourself weight machine. "That's quite a contraption you've got there."

Good ol' Mr. Dad. He'd seen all of our inventions . . . the Hydro-Powered Pencil Sharpener, the Jet-Powered Alarm Clock, the Remote-Control Clothes Dryer, and our infamous Make-You-Think-We're-in-the-Room-When-We're-Really-Out-Catching-a-Flick-We-Shouldn't-Be-Catching Answering

Machine. But no matter what the invention, he always played it cool and pretended they were just something you'd expect from your average, run-of-the-mill, intellectual genius types.

"Thanks." Nick nodded as he accepted the compliment. "Of course, Thurman has a real weight machine at his house." Good ol' Nick. As an official kid he knows the value of throwing in a little guilt to make his parents feel he's deprived. It never hurts to build up those guilt reserves for future causes.

"I'm not surprised," Mr. Dad said, neatly side-stepping the guilt trap. "Guys like Thurman always set a winning example. Hey," he added as he crawled underneath the bar and cords of the weight machine. "Put another couple of books on this thing."

"Sure," Nick agreed.

As Mr. Dad finished sliding into place, Nick grabbed volumes L and M of the encyclopedias to throw on the machine.

"You know, Nick, this ball game really means a lot to me," he said. Then, suddenly remembering he was a parent and above such childish desires as wanting to stomp Harvey the Snorter, Mr. Dad started over. "Er, that is, this ball game means a lot to all of us." He motioned for Nicholas to toss the N and O-P volumes onto the weight pile, too. "In a game like this," he continued, "everybody's got to pull their weight to win."

Nick nodded as he plopped the volumes onto the pile, which was getting bigger by the second. Mr. Dad glanced at the pile, then motioned to Nick. "Go ahead," he insisted. "I can handle more than that." He was obviously in one of his more macho moods.

Nicholas gave the pile a dubious look. Then, after a shrug, grabbed Q-R, S and T, and tossed them onto the pile as well.

At last Mr. Dad gave the bar a pull.

Nothing.

He pulled the bar a little harder.

Repeat performance. The weights wouldn't budge. He cleared his throat, frowned in concentration, and tried again.

Same results. Nothing moved—not a fraction.

Most dads would have been pretty embarrassed by now. But always in charge, and always the one to set the good example, Mr. Dad quickly changed the subject. "Well, this has been fun, but I'd better get going. Things are pretty hectic right now, so I'm really too busy to lift weights." It was an old ploy, one of the first they teach you in Dad School, and he pulled it off like a pro. "But don't worry, I'll, uh, I'll help you with your weights some other time."

For a moment Nick was confused. Then, he broke into a smile. He knew exactly what was going on. "Sure, Dad," he said with a grin.

"Anyway, what I was trying to say about the game," Mr. Dad continued as he attempted to climb out of the machine (somehow getting in was a lot easier than getting out), "what I was trying to say is that you and the other guys need to turn it up a notch. Thurman's got to have support on the mound, so I need you to give it all you have this week, OK?"

"Right, Dad."

Still struggling to untangle himself from the bar and cords, Mr. Dad nodded and added, "The other guys, too."

"Sure, Dad."

More struggling. "I mean I really want to win this one."

"Absolutely, Dad."

Finally, just when Nick was starting to wonder if he'd have to step in and give his dad a hand, Mr. Dad managed to untangle himself and get out. His hair looked like he was doing an Einstein imitation, and his clothes were all cockeyed, but he still managed to look down to Nick with a fatherly, I-know-exactly-what-I'm-doing grin. "That's great, Son," he said, patting Nick on the shoulder. "I knew you'd understand."

Nick tried not to smile.

Then with one last pat and a little hair tousling thrown in for good measure, Mr. Dad turned and headed out of the room, all the time trying to rub out the aches that had suddenly appeared in his shoulders.

Nicholas looked after him, smiling. He loved his dad. And he respected him . . . weaknesses and all.

FIVE
"'Cause It's Root, Root, Root for the Home Team. . . ."

The following day everybody got up nice and early to get to practice. And I do mean *early*. In fact, Nick got up so early that for the first time in his life he was able to get into the bathroom before his sisters. It was a strange sensation seeing an absolutely spotless counter—no eyeliners, eyeshadows, or lipsticks scattered across its surface. There wasn't even the usual array of rouge, baby powder, hair dryers, and electric curlers. It was even stranger not having to scrape off the layer of hair spray that normally collected on the mirror during Sarah's multiple coats of hair varnish. Strangest of all was not having his nose twitch and itch over the nauseating aromas of bath oils, shampoos, and perfumes.

The sun was just peeking over the trees as the bleary-eyed team stumbled onto the field for a torturous workout. It wasn't that Dad was interested in winning or anything like that. He just wanted to make sure that there was absolutely no way in heaven or on earth, by accident or on purpose, on land or sea, by gosh or by golly, that Harvey the Snorter's team would come anywhere close to beating them again.

"All right, everybody," Dad clapped as he cheered the kids onto the field. "Heads up, look alive now."

The kids looked anything but "alive" as they staggered toward their positions. Everyone was still groggy and half asleep. Well, almost everyone.

Thurman Miller had been up for hours. He had to be to squeeze in his weight lifting, his four-mile run, and his three glasses of Macho-Muscle Protein Drink.

"Right, Coach!" he bellowed as he dropped down to do a dozen squat thrusts for warm-up.

Nicholas and Louis stared. Amazing. This was their hero. This was the guy they dreamed of imitating—and he was doing warm-ups in the middle of the night without even being asked! Crazy. Absurd. Loony Tunes. So Loony Tunes that Nicholas and Louis glanced at each other and, without a word, dropped down to join him. What other choice did they have?

A little later, Thurman, all decked out with wristbands, a batting glove, and a billion pieces of Big Chew bubble gum stuffed into his cheek, stepped up to the plate. He gave a few practice swings and calmly waited to start bashing the ball out of the park.

Off to the side, Nicholas and Louis were also putting on their wristbands and batting gloves (which just happened to be the same style and color as Thurman's).

"The left hand," Nicholas whispered.

Louis looked up. "Huh?"

"The left hand. Your batting glove goes on the *left* hand."

Louis shot a look over to Thurman. Nick was right. Their hero was wearing it on his left hand. Quickly the boy changed hands.

"Got any Big Chew?" Nicholas asked.

"Naw." Louis shrugged as he pulled the empty pouch from his pocket. "I gave the last of it to Thurman."

For a moment Nick was lost. How could he be like Thurman Miller if he didn't have any Big Chew? If Thurman Miller had Big Chew, then Nicholas Martin would need Big Chew. It was a simple fact.

Finally a simple solution came to mind. Without a second thought, Nicholas wadded up the empty pouch, popped it into his mouth and stuffed it into one of his cheeks. Now he looked just like Thurman Miller. It was a brilliant idea. At least until he noticed the taste. Then he couldn't spit the pouch out fast enough.

"Cool." Louis smirked as Nick continued to cough and spit. "Real cool."

"Hey, you guys!" Thurman called.

Immediately both boys spun around.

"Hit the outfield for some flies!"

Say no more. His wish was their command. They grabbed their gloves and raced toward the field.

Meanwhile, Dad was concentrating on the statistics on his clipboard. All yesterday evening he had been working up strategies. All night he had been dreaming about them. All day today he would be working them out. It wasn't an easy job, but it was one of the many things that had to be done to make sure Harvey the Snorter didn't stand a chance of winning.

Suddenly there were three loud snorts followed by obnoxious laughter. Dad cringed. He knew what would happen next. And, sure enough, just like clockwork, Harvey the Snorter's big clumsy hand crashed down on Dad's shoulder . . . a little too hard and a little too friendly.

"Hey, Dave!" the big man shouted just a little too loudly. "How's the *second* best manager in the league?"

"Fine, just fine," Dad said, doing his best imitation of a smile, which ended up being more grimace than grin. "Good to see you, Harvey." OK, so it wasn't exactly the truth, but Dad didn't want to hurt the big guy's feelings. Then, out of the corner of his eye, Dad noticed Thurman smashing the ball to the fielders. Come to think of it, maybe he *was* telling the truth . . . maybe he *was* glad to see Harvey.

Harvey snorted again as he gave Dad another big slap on the back. "You know, Dave, considering last year's massacre, no one would blame you if you forfeited the game this Saturday." He broke out with a wheezy laugh. "I mean, you'd sure save us all a lot of trouble." He ended with a couple more snorts.

Once again Thurman laid into the ball. And once again Nicholas and Louis watched as it sailed high over their heads and out of the park.

This time Harvey noticed it, too. "Hey, nice hitting. Who's your assistant?"

It was Dad's turn to grin. No grimace this time. It was a real, legitimate grin. "That's Thurman Miller. . . ." He hesitated a second, savoring the moment. Then finally he finished, "my *pitcher*."

"Your *what!?*"

Thurman smashed another ball, and it sailed high over Nick's head and out of the park. Thurman had cost the team a fortune in baseballs, but right now Dad figured it was worth every penny.

Harvey the Snorter watched in stunned amazement.

"What's the matter, Harv?" Dad teased. "You look kinda pale."

Harvey the Snorter tried to answer, but he could only stare as Thurman prepared to hit another ball.

Dad continued the dig. "I hope you're not coming down with anything. You know, like *chicken* pox. . . ."

Thurman smacked another.

At last Harvey the Snorter was able to speak as he fumbled for his glasses. "Whattaya trying to pull, Martin?" he sputtered, slipping on the spectacles for a better look. "That guy played Triple-A for the Cubs last season! I'm sure of it!"

Dad's grin was looking more and more like the Cheshire cat's. "He's thirteen years old," he gloated. "And he meets all the Little League requirements. What else do you want to know, Sherlock?"

Thurman clobbered another one out of the park.

By now, Harvey was no longer snorting. Instead he was starting to stutter. "You, you wantta get ugly?" he finally managed to blurt out. "I . . . I can get ugly."

"I'll bet you can," Dad agreed.

"I've got a few surprises, too, Martin. We'll see who has the last laugh—just like last year!"

"Last year is history, pal. Just like your winning streak."

"Oh . . . oh, yeah?" Harvey the Snorter demanded.

"Catchy comeback, Harv. We'll see you Saturday." With that, Dad dismissed the man and turned to watch Thurman clobber another ball out of the park.

Harvey the Snorter would have stuck around to watch, but he had other things to do—like storm to his car, like drive to the nearest Golden Arches, and like eat himself into oblivion—something the man always did when he was upset. And today he was real upset: three Big Macs, two sides of fries, and four chocolate shakes' worth of upset.

Meanwhile, Nicholas and Louis were still out in the field watching balls sail over their heads.

"See that cloud, there?" Nick asked. "It's kinda shaped like the trophy we're gonna win at the Regionals. . . ."

But Louis wasn't watching the clouds, he was watching another Thurman Miller special shoot high into orbit. "Man, how'd you like to be able to hit like that?"

Still staring at the clouds, Nicholas nodded. Although his eyes were on the clouds, his mind was already a million miles away, experiencing another world-famous Nicholas Martin fantasy. . . .

"Next up," the announcer's voice reverberated about the stadium. "It's Slam-the-Man Martin, the greatest home-run hitter of all time!"

Immediately the crowd of 1.3 million spectators (hey, it's Nick's fantasy—he can have as many people as he wants) was on its feet cheering. Next it began to chant: "Mar-tin! Mar-tin! Mar-tin!"

Finally, the mighty Slam Martin stepped out of the dugout. A tremendous roar filled the stadium. Strangely enough, Slam-the-Man was decked out exactly like Thurman Miller, to the very last detail. Of course, the muscles looked a little phony, but it was the best Nick could dream up on such short notice. This time he had some real Big Chew in his mouth. Yes sir, no fooling around now. Slam Martin was ready to be a world-famous hero . . . again.

He gave a wink to the TV cameras, waved to the president and first lady, then strolled toward the plate. The bases were loaded. All they needed was one little ol' grand slam, and they would win. By now the roar was deafening as Slam took a couple practice swings and waited.

For a moment he felt a twinge of pity for the pitcher. It was Orel Hershiser. Poor guy. He may be the greatest pitcher known to man, but his great greatness was no match for the greatness of the great Slam Martin.

Orel knew it, too. I mean the guy was sweating like a Sumo wrestler in a sauna. Obviously he knew he didn't stand a chance—mainly because he knew whose daydream this was. But he had no choice—he had to go through with the game. Finally he took a deep breath and began the windup.

Slam crouched low and waited.

Orel fired the ball. It was the best pitch of his life. The crowd gasped in awe, but you could barely hear it over the sonic boom the ball made as it broke the sound barrier and rocketed toward Martin.

But Slam wasn't worried. In fact, he did his best to stifle a yawn as the supersonic projectile hurtled toward him at a zillion miles an hour. At first Slam wasn't sure what to do: Did he want to hit a home run or just a triple? After all, he liked Orel and didn't want to embarrass the guy too much. Then he remembered that the fate of the entire free world rested on this one pitch. (Apparently our president and the secretary general of the Soviet Union had a little bet riding on the game. Something about a title deed to North America. . . .)

So Slam Martin leaned back and swung.

K-THWAK!

The ball sailed high, higher, and even higher until it was completely out of sight. In fact, it sailed so high that one of the umpires had to go in and call air traffic control just to keep track of it on radar. The crowd was going crazy as Slam trotted around the bases and followed the other runners home. Everyone raced onto the field, hoisted him to their shoulders, then carried him into the locker room to celebrate.

Everything was going perfect. Well, almost everything. There was one little catch. No one had really figured that the ball would hit the bottom of a high-flying 747 and bounce directly back into the park. But, of course, that's exactly what happened. Before Slam and the other runners were able to get out of the locker room and back onto their bases, the center fielder caught the returning ball and fired it around the infield for a triple play.

The crowd booed. Then it hissed. Then it booed and hissed.

The great Slam Martin hung his head in shame. Why had he been so careless, so overconfident? A real pro would have expected something like that to happen.

"Don't feel too bad, Slam." The boy looked up. It was Orel walking beside him, putting his arm around him. "There's more to life than winning. Besides, no single player can expect to do it all. It takes a whole team to win a game."

Suddenly Orel's voice began to sound sneakingly familiar . . . and suddenly Nick's daydream began to dissolve. He was back in the Little League field watching a fly ball finish rolling to a stop at his feet.

"Come on, it takes a whole team to win a game!" It was Dad shouting. "Let's wake up out there! Come on now, we have a long way to go!"

Well, so much for another sensational Nicholas Martin daydream.

But Dad was right. They did have a long way to go. Longer than either father or son could imagine. . . .

SIX
"If They Don't Win It's a Shame. . . ."

Yes-siree-bob, ol' Nicky-boy and his pop were pretty serious about winning. Too serious, if you ask me. It's like I always say, "It's not whether you win or lose that counts, it's how bad Thurman demolishes your opponent." No, no, no, that's what they've been saying. What I say is, "It's not whether you win or lose that counts, it's who gets to eat all the popcorn and hot dogs left over after the concession stand closes." Well, that's not exactly right either . . . but I think you get the picture.

Of course, what I really wanted was for my little buddy to see what was really happening—to understand that he was putting too much stock in Thurman. And I was kinda curious where he thought God fit into all of this . . . assuming he'd thought about God at all lately. But hey, I had more important things to do than throw these questions at my buddy—like getting my hands on his Ryne Sandberg baseball card!

We were up in his room, and I had just offered him my favorite Slimy Cleavus card. You know Slimy, the world-famous cartoon outfielder and part-time used-car salesman? It was my best offer, but Nick just wasn't biting.

"Who's this guy supposed to be?" he demanded.

"Who's he supposed to be?! Are you kidding? Slimy is headed for the Hall of Fame!"

43

"Right," Nicholas scoffed. "The Geek Hall of Fame."

I was obviously ringing up a No Sale with Nick, so it was time to put all my cards on the table . . . literally.

"All right," I said as I fanned the rest of my baseball cards out onto his bed. "I'll even throw in Oxo Nubbins."

Nick just looked at me. Man! Talk about driving a hard bargain!

"OK, OK, how 'bout Slats Felldoe?"

"Slats Felldoe?" he asked incredulously. It was pretty obvious he didn't know much about the National Cartoon League.

OK, kid, tell ya what I'm gonna do. In trade for your Ryne Sandberg, you can be the proud owner of Slimy Cleavus and Otho Mounds . . . a legend in his own grime!"

"McGee," he said with a sigh.

All right! He was finally starting to weaken. He was finally starting to see reason. He was finally starting to . . .

"Get a brain, will ya?"

. . . get on my nerves. I had no choice. He left me no alternative. Now it was time to mesmerize him with my marvelously magnificent McGeeisms. I grabbed a nearby pencil and took a few practice swings. "I tell you, Buddy-Boy, that Cleavus had one mean swing." I pulled an imaginary ball from my back pocket, the one I keep there for just such occasions. Tossing it into the air, I did my best Cleavus swing and smacked that sphere to Saturn. Well, almost . . .

First it got Nick's lamp—ZING!
Then it decked his dinosaur—ZONG!
Then it nailed the world globe—ZANG!
Then it ricocheted off the mirror—ZUNG!
Then it clobbered me on the bean—OUCH!
Suddenly the room was full of stars . . . and we ain't talkin'

Sylvester the cat here. I staggered this way and that, that way and this. Then I felt this strange urge to lie down. It wasn't like I was tired or anything like that, but I'd heard it's the in thing to do when you're knocked unconscious. And, not wanting to be out of style, I followed suit. . . .

CRASH-BOOM!

Fortunately Nick was right there at my side. As usual, he tried to help me with his gentle kindness, his tender concern, and his quiet words of encouragement: "I hope you have baseball out of your system now, Pine Tar Breath!"

His gentle bedside manner was all it took. Immediately I was back on my feet. "Are you kidding?" I argued. "And give up all that fame and fortune?" Already I could hear the clanking of change, the grabbing of greenbacks, the swishing of savings certificates. "Big leagues mean big bucks," I insisted. "Just in endorsements alone!"

To prove my point, I let go with a lightning-like leap landing me lightly on the lad's lap. (Say that three times fast.) Nick grabbed his pencil, reached for his sketch pad, and let me hop onto the paper. Then, before you could say, "Uh-oh, here comes another fantasy," I was starring in one of those superjock commercials.

Hmm, looks like I'm in some old black-and-white newsreel footage. It's back in my "good ol' days," when I was playing center field for the New York Hankies. And what's old black-and-white footage without some old-time, play-by-play announcing?

"Ladies and gentlemen, you should hear the roar of this crowd out here in Mile Sty Stadium. Slugger Stan Steroid steps to the plate. There's the windup, the pitch and . . . the Steroid slams another one toward center field!

"Center fielder McGee drops back . . . back . . . this one may be out of here folks! Now McGee's on the warning track, now he jumps and . . . what a sensational catch! McGee leaps high over the fence, stealing a homer and the winning run from the Steroid Kid! Just listen to this crowd!"

Suddenly, we're pulling back from the TV monitor, and there I am again, only thirty years later. Man alive, what a bod, what a face, and what terrific acting. Just listen. . . .

"Yes sir, that was . . . uh, I mean, that was me, yeah me, back in . . . don't tell me, oh yeah, 1962. Pretty impressive, huh? But these, uh, I mean . . . that is to say, these days I call the, uh, the big plays, uh, behind the mike in the, what do you call it, oh yeah, the press box and, uh, er, uh, I . . ."

OK, OK, I know I sound a little stiff, but I get better. Just keep watching.

"And, after uh, oh yeah, after a hard day . . . phew . . . I like to freshen up with a little, a little splash of Old Lice After-Shave."

Pretty good job, huh? And look what a great job I'm doing of holding the bottle up to the camera. And look how fast I'm turning it around so it's right side up. What a pro. Shhh . . . I've got one more line.

"Yes sir! Get some Old Lice . . . for the louse in your life!"

I glanced up at Nick from the sketch pad. "What do you think, kiddo?"

"Nah," Nick said as he ripped out the page and started drawing again. . . .

Oh, hey, this is even better. Now I'm lounging around the pool. There must be a thousand-and-one beautiful gals hanging *around. Obviously just a small cross section of my many adoring fans. Oh, wait, I'm getting ready to speak. . . .*

"Ya know, these days when I work up a big thirst, I like to quench it with an ice-cold Canine Cola."

All right! Check out the big grin I'm giving to the camera as I'm reaching past the bag of Ava's Pork Rinds to the can that, of course, has a picture of a big dog on it. Now I'm chugging it down, and instead of a burp out comes a mighty "WOOF!!"

Then, of course, I have to give the little wink to the camera. And let's not forget the ever-popular jingle. Talk about original!

"Drink Canine Cola, la-la-la . . . it's doggone good. WOOF!"

Wow! What a masterpiece! What perfection. Look out, Academy Awards, here I come.

I glanced up at Nicholas and was going to congratulate him on a job well done, but the kid wasn't smiling. Apparently he still felt it wasn't quite right.

Artists—who can figure 'em?

He ripped out the page and tried for one last commercial. . . .

Ahhh, this is more like it. I'm in my rugged outdoorsman uniform. You know, the one with the plaid shirt, cuffed jeans, and the ever-popular, steel-toed logging boots. And speaking of logging, that's me cutting down that tree. My oh my, look how I swing that ax . . .

SCHUNK! . . . SCHUNK! . . . SCHUNK!

Now I'm dusting the manly dust from my manly hands and

looking at the camera, giving my marvelously manly smile. As I start walking toward my new pickup I begin to talk. . . .

"Y'know, when I played ball, it was a tough game. But not as tough as the payments on my new Shimmy Truck."

I give the ol' Shimmy a pat on the side before climbing in.

Now we cut to the next scene, and I'm heading down a steep mountain road, the truck bouncing and shimmying like Jell-O on a jackhammer. I try to talk but the vibrations are pretty strong. . . .

"A-n-d-d-d y-y-y-ou t-t-t-alk-k-k a-b-b-b-out t-t-t-ough . . ."

I seem to be picking up too much speed, so I try the brakes. Funny, they don't seem to be working as well as they should. Come to think of it, they're not working at all! But that's OK, I'm a professional. I can still say my lines. . . .

"Y-y-y-ou ough-t-t-t to s-s-s-ee the wa-ay-ay-ay this b-b-b-ab-b-b-y hand-d-d-dles."

Things are starting to get serious. I'm going so fast that the trees on one side are a blur. If I hit any of them it could really smart—not to mention mess up my fabulously combed hair. Fortunately there are no trees on the other side. Just a 358-foot drop-off.

A 358-FOOT DROP-OFF?!

OK, OK, that's no problem for a cool, in-control superstar athlete like myself. I'll just downshift. I'll just take this old gearshift here and . . .

GRIND! GRIND! GRIND!

Hmm, must be something wrong with the clutch. Maybe if I just pump it a little . . .

PUMP! PUMP! PUMP!

Uh-oh . . .

GRIND! GRIND! GRIND!

PUMP! PUMP! PUMP!

Did you ever have one of those days?

Faster and faster I race down the road. But never being one to lose my head—I clear my throat and calmly scream:

"N I C H O L A S! I D-D-D-ON'T LI-I-I-I-KE THIS-S-S COM-M-M-M-ERCIAL!!"

Nicky-boy doesn't seem to hear. By now everything is a blur—the trees, the road, even the handwriting on this Last Will and Testament I'm quickly throwing together! In fact, the only thing racing past my eyes faster than the trees and the highway is my life.

Any second now I'll be flying off this cliff. Any second now I'll be heading for that great sketch pad in the sky. Suddenly, like music to my ears, I hear Nick's mom. "Nicholas, come on down for dinner."

Then comes an even better tune: "OK, Mom."

Suddenly everything froze. Nick was done sketching. I looked up to see his grinning face.

"Don't go anywhere, Mop-Top," he chirped as he tossed his art pencil over to the table. "I'll be back after dinner."

"Take all the time you need," I managed to croak. "Maybe afterward Sarah would like some help with the dishes. Oh, and maybe you could help pack Jamie's lunch for tomorrow. Come to think of it, the kitchen could stand a little remodeling, too!"

But he was gone.

And, as soon as I can jimmy this truck door open, I'll be gone, too. Ah, there we go.

Now if I can just find out where he threw that sketch of the pool with the ladies, soda, and pork rinds. . . .

SEVEN
"'Cause It's One, Two, Three Strikes . . ."

The last few days before the game were just like the others
. . . only worse.

Nick and Louis continued to fall all over themselves as
they waited on Thurman hand and foot. I mean, they
were doing everything but bowing and calling him "Master." Thurman's slightest wish had become their command. No. Better make that Thurman's slightest whim of
a wish had become their command.

And Dad, poor Dad, wasn't doing much better. It
seems all he did was think and plan and develop strategies for the upcoming game. When he wasn't thinking
and planning he was gloating—over the final destruction
of Harvey the Snorter. Yes sir, it was going to be sweet.

On the day before the big game Nicholas brought
Thurman over for a little snack. Sarah was sitting at the table
going through the mail when the kitchen door flew open
and in swaggered Nicholas and his incredible bulky buddy.

Quickly Nick pulled out a chair so the big guy could
have a seat. Which put Thurman right in front of Sarah.
She looked up and smiled. So this was the superjock
everybody was so ga-ga over. She continued to smile,
waiting for some sort of introduction.

Not a word was said.

Sarah waited some more.

Still nothing.

Now the corners around her smile were starting to droop. Somebody better say something. She couldn't keep this smile on forever. But it was becoming more and more obvious that no one was going to say anything. Finally, in an effort to show some sort of friendliness, she cleared her throat and offered a "Hi."

Thurman looked up, surprised. Apparently he hadn't even noticed she was in the room, even though they were only three feet from each other.

"Oh, hi, ahhh. . . ." He was fumbling for a name, any name.

"Sarah," she offered.

"Right." Thurman nodded, acting like he knew it all along.

By now Nick had crossed to the fridge and was peering inside. "Looks like we got chicken salad, apples, meatloaf, banana bread—"

"That'd be fine," Thurman agreed.

Once again Sarah looked up.

"All of it?" Nick asked.

"Sure," Thurman said with a shrug.

Sarah tried to return to her mail. It was a pretty good batch. One letter even said she was a grand prize winner. All she had to do was come down and claim that prize . . . and of course listen to a ninety-minute sales presentation on mobile home vacation campsites on beautiful Lake Hackneehoho. Suddenly Sarah began to suspect junk mail wasn't all it was cracked up to be. So she put all that aside to watch Thurman.

Nick returned to the table, balancing three plates and two bowls. "Here you go," he said as he quickly spread everything before the human eating machine.

Thurman dug in—sometimes chewing, sometimes swallowing . . . but most of the time just inhaling.

Sarah looked on, horrified. Well, horrified *and* fascinated.

Thurman, with his mouth stuffed fuller than humanly possible, began motioning for something to drink.

"Right," Nick said, jumping back to his feet. He raced to the fridge to take another inventory. "We've got cola, chocolate milk, O. J. . . ."

"OK," Thurman mumbled through the chicken salad, apples, and meatloaf.

"All of the above?" Sarah asked dryly. Up until now she had been able to keep quiet. But expecting an older sister to keep her mouth shut through all of this would be as likely as expecting her to fold your socks on wash day.

Thurman grinned. A thick layer of banana bread coated his front teeth. He didn't want Sarah to think he was a pig about the drinks so he compromised. "Cola'd be fine," he called as he caught a piece of chicken trying to escape from the left corner of his mouth.

Immediately Nicholas was at his side, pouring a nice tall glass of cola.

"Where's the ice?" Thurman asked.

"Oh. Right. Ice," Nick answered as he spun around and raced for the freezer compartment of the fridge.

Sarah watched with amazement as Nick threw open the

door, fumbled for the ice tray, and fought to pull the handle on it. It was frozen stuck. "Maybe Thurman can help you with that," she offered sarcastically.

Nick was too busy to hear the sarcasm. "No way!" he insisted as he wrestled with the tray, using every bit of strength he had. "Thurman could strain his arm or cut his hand or—OUCH!" Nick stuffed his pinched finger into his mouth and sucked hard to fight off the pain. But pain was no obstacle. Not when it came to pleasing the great Thurman Miller. "We can't have Thurman injured the day before the big game," he insisted.

"Heaven forbid," Sarah muttered under her breath. But before she could say anything more she was interrupted by a huge slurp of cola followed by a gigantic burp.

"Well, thanks, Nick" the human garbage disposal said as he scooted his chair back and slowly rose to his feet. "Gotta go. Hey, did ya get all the dirt out of my cleats?"

Nicholas beamed proudly. "You could eat off those cleats."

"But don't try," Sarah threw in, "you might chip a tooth."

"Yeah, uh, right," Thurman answered, not getting the joke. He turned and started out the door. "See ya tomorrow, Nick."

Nick gave him his best grin.

"And uh, we'll see ya later, uh . . . Karen."

But before Sarah could correct him, the door slammed and he was gone.

It took Sarah a moment to find her voice. "That was unbelievable!" she finally exclaimed.

By now Nicholas had scooped up Thurman's dishes

and was dumping them into the sink. "Yeah," he agreed, "he sure can eat."

"I'll say," she marveled. "He practically—" Then she caught herself. "No . . . I'm not talking about the way he ate . . . I'm talking about the way you fell all over yourself for him! It just doesn't seem right."

"Look," Nicholas argued. "Thurman's like a . . . you know, like a star!"

Sarah could only stare. She had seen Nick get carried away before but never quite like this.

"Yeah, a star," Nick repeated as he began rinsing the dishes. "You should be proud he even stopped by for a bite."

"A bite?! Godzilla would have done less damage."

Nick could only sigh. How could a big sister that's supposed to be so smart be so dumb?

"Nick." Now she was trying to reason. "Isn't it possible that you're so caught up with Thurman as a baseball player that you can't see what he's like as a person?"

Again Nicholas let out a sigh. It wasn't a great defense, but it was about the only one he had.

Sarah did her best to make him see the light. "Don't get me wrong," she tried to explain. "I mean, it's OK to admire someone. . . . But you . . . Nick, you worship the guy. You treat him like he's some kind of idol. And the guy's not even nice!"

"What's being nice got to do with it?"

"Nick . . ."

Nicholas had had just about enough. Sarah was obviously in one of her preaching moods, and there would be no reasoning with her. So he turned off the water and headed for the stairs.

"Nick, answer me. . . . Nicholas!"

Finally he turned back to her. She wanted an answer? All right, he'd give her an answer. "You're just jealous," he shot back. "You're jealous because we're about to become regional champs! And you, all you have going for you right now is . . ." He looked around until his eyes landed on the letters in front of her: "Mail!"

Sarah wasn't fazed. In fact, there was something about her that was really sincere. This was more important than their usual brother and sister spats. And she was going to get through to him, no matter how much he tried to hurt her.

"I'm not jealous, Nick." She swallowed hard, then she laid out all the cards. "I'm not jealous . . . but maybe God is."

Nick threw her a look. But she continued.

"*God's* supposed to be the center of our attention," she explained quietly, "He's the one we're supposed to trust . . . remember?"

"Yeah, right, sure," Nicholas countered, not wanting to hear any more. Sarah was starting to make sense, and that was the last thing he wanted or needed. "Just you wait!" he said. "After tomorrow you'll be telling all your friends that Thurman Miller actually spoke to you . . . *Karen!*"

Before Sarah could respond, Nick turned and stormed up the stairs. She watched after him for a long moment. There must be some way she could get through to him—some way she could show him the problem.

Then again, maybe she couldn't. Maybe it would take Someone bigger and better and more loving. Maybe it would take that very Person who wanted to be the center of all of Nick's trust. . . .

EIGHT
"You're Out!"

At last the day of the big game arrived. We're not just talking big game, mind you, we're talking BIG GAME. The
Eastfield Braves against the Dodgers. Since Dad ran the
local paper, he made sure every radio and TV station in
the state knew what was happening. Nothing would
please him more than for the whole world to see Harvey
the Snorter go down in flames.

Nicholas also had gone to a few extremes, like having
Mom wash his uniform three times just in case there were
any hidden grass stains he hadn't seen. Then there was
the matter of his shoes. He tried and tried to clean up all
the scuffs, but nothing seemed to work . . . that is until
Louis loaned him his can of white spray paint. Now they
were all set. Now nobody would be able to stop them. . . .

"Come on, you're doggin' it!" Dad shouted at his team
during the warm-ups in the field. "Do you want to win?"

"Yes!" they shouted.

"Do you want to win?"

"Yes!"

"DO YOU WANT TO WIN?"

"YES!!"

Up in the bleachers Mom, Grandma, Jamie, and Sarah

exchanged uneasy glances. They wanted to win, too. But somehow the man shouting at those kids down there was not the same gentle man they loved and respected. Somehow something had happened. In fact, at that moment he seemed a lot like . . . Harvey the Snorter.

"Let's bash 'em!" Harvey was shouting.

"Yes sir!"

"Let's stomp 'em!"

"Yes sir!"

"LET'S TROMP 'EM!"

"YES SIR!"

"Let's play ball!" the umpire shouted.

Dad's team, the Braves, took the field first. A cheer rose up from the crowd as Thurman stalked toward the pitcher's mound and took his stance. Everyone knew what was about to happen . . . especially the frightened batter who was first up for the Dodgers.

Thurman glanced at his watch, stifled a yawn, and started his windup. Exactly two minutes and 24 seconds later, Thurman was heading back to the dugout. He had struck out three batters with three sizzling fast balls apiece! "Can't do any better than that," he boasted.

But the Dodger pitcher was almost as good as Thurman. And by the third inning the score was still:

Braves—0
Dodgers—0

Then, almost by accident, a Dodger connected with one of Thurman's curves. Unfortunately little Roger Goreman, the wanna-be film director, was playing shortstop. Even more unfortunately, the ball headed directly for him. Now little Roger had two choices, either play it safe and dodge the oncoming ball or try to catch it. Not being one to take too many chances, ol' Roger decided to leap out of the way.

But the ball still managed to hit him, and by the time he found it and picked it up, the batter was nearly to first.

"Throw it! Throw it!" the first baseman yelled.

Roger threw it. Unfortunately he missed his mark by about fifteen feet and everyone watched as the ball sailed high into the grandstands.

Meanwhile, the runner, who could have come into second standing up, thought it would be great to show off with a little slide . . . a slide that knocked second baseman Louis off his feet and high into the air.

Immediately Dad was out on the field shouting about the unnecessary roughness, and immediately one of the umpires was in his face shouting at him to cool it.

Mom glanced away, embarrassed.

Thurman was so upset because the kid got a double off him that he walked the next three runners and hit the fourth. Finally, after a little talk on the pitcher's mound, Dad was able to settle him down to finish the inning. But the damage was already done. The score at the end of the third inning was:

Braves—0
Dodgers—2

By the fifth inning, Nick had struck out once and grounded out once. Now he was up to bat again. Things would be different this time. Dad had given him a big pep talk just before he left the dugout, and now the kid was ready to do some major damage. He stepped into the batting box, took a few manly practice swings, and did his best to look mean and ferocious at the pitcher.

Three swings and three strikes later, Nick was heading back to the dugout, having done no damage and definitely not feeling all that mean or ferocious.

Dad was not pleased with Nick and showed it.

Mom was not pleased with Dad and tried not to show it.

Harvey was pleased with everyone and snorted in glee.

Things got even more interesting for the next three innings. Dad's team pressed in hard and actually managed to score five runs! Two of them were courtesy of Thurman Miller's mighty biceps; the other three came from kids lucky enough to be on base when those biceps belted out their homers. It was incredible . . . terrific . . . fantastic!

The only problem was Harvey's team had also scored five more runs. It was awful . . . unbelievable . . . dreadful!

The score by the end of the eighth inning was:

Braves—5
Dodgers—7

Finally the ninth inning rolled around. Dad's team was still behind by two runs, but any second now they were expecting—

Hold it. Wait a minute, Bub. What say we let a real storyteller tell this tallish tale, shall we? After all, I was there. I saw it, I heard it, I lived it. Yes sir, you guessed it—it is I, the world-famous poet, Henry Wadsworth McGeefellow. Being such a famous former of phrases and a renown wrangler of rhymes, what better way for me to tell this epic story than with a praiseworthy poem?

So, sit back and get ready for some real culture.

Ahem . . . Ladies and gentlemen, guys and guyettes, it is with dynamically dramatic talent (and sincerely apologetic apologies to the real poet, Earnest Lawrence Thayer), that I recite "Casey—", er, make that "Thurman at the Bat."

> "It looked extremely rocky for the Eastfield nine that
>   day;
> The score stood 5 to 7 with an inning left to play.
> So, when Eddie died at second, and Peter did the
>   same,
> A pallor weathered the features of the patrons of the
>   game.
>
> "A straggling few got up to go *[those rotten, no-good
>   traitors]*, leaving there the rest,
> With that hope that springs eternal within the
>   human breast.
> For they thought: 'If only Thurman could get a crack
>   at that,'
> They'd put money even now, with Thurman at the
>   bat."

Pretty good so far, huh? Hang on, it gets better . . .

"Then Nick let drive a single, to the wonderment of
   all.
And the understated Louis tore the cover off the
   ball.
And when the dust had lifted and they saw what had
   occurred,
There was Louis safe at second and Nick a-huggin'
   third."

Atta baby, Nick! All right, Louis! Nice work guys!

"Then from the gladdened multitude went up a joy-
   ous yell—
It rumbled in the mountaintops, it rattled in the
   dell;
It struck upon the hillside and rebounded on the
   flat;
For Thurman, mighty Thurman, was advancing to
   the bat."

All right, Thurmmy!

"There was ease in Thurman's manner as he stepped
   into his place,
There was pride in Thurman's bearing and a smile
   upon his face;
And when responding to the cheers he lightly tipped
   his hat,
No stranger in the crowd could doubt it's Thurman
   at the bat.

"Ten thousand eyes were on him . . . ."

OK, so there were only three or four hundred. Haven't you ever heard of poetic license?

"Ten thousand eyes were on him . . . as he rubbed
  his hands with dirt,
Five thousand tongues applauded when he wiped
  them on his shirt;
Then when the writhing pitcher ground the ball into
  his hip,
Defiance glanced in Thurman's eye, a sneer curled
  Thurman's lip.

"And now the leather-covered sphere came hurtling
  through the air,
And Thurman stood a-watching it in haughty gran-
  deur there.
Close by the sturdy batsman the ball unheeded sped
  [the puppy was flying!];
'That ain't my style,' said Thurman. 'Strike one,' the
  umpire said.

"From the benches full of people, there went up a
  muffled roar,
Like the beating of the storm waves on the stern and
  distant shore.
'Kill him! Kill the umpire!' shouted someone on the
  stand;
And it's likely they'd have killed him had not
  Thurman raised his hand.

"With a smile of noble charity great Thurman's vis-
   age shone [translation: The guy was cool.];
He stilled the rising tumult, he made the game go
   on;
He signaled to the pitcher, and once more the spher-
   oid flew;
But Thurman still ignored it, and the umpire said,
   'Strike two.'

"'Fraud!' cried the maddened thousands, and the
   echo answered 'Fraud!'
But one scornful look from Thurman, and the audience was awed;
They saw his face grow stern and cold, they saw his
   muscles strain,
And they knew that Thurman wouldn't let the ball
   go by again.

"The sneer is gone from Thurman's lips, his teeth are
   clenched in hate,
He pounds with cruel vengeance his bat upon the
   plate;
And now the pitcher holds the ball, and now he lets
   it go,
And now the air is shattered by the force of
   Thurman's blow . . ."

*And blow it did. I tell you, when that guy finished swinging it
was like a minihurricane. Hats blew away, and toupees blew
off. It was incredible! But not incredible enough. Let's see,
where was I? Oh, yeah . . .*

"Oh, somewhere in this favored land the sun is
    shining bright,
The band is playing somewhere, and somewhere
    hearts are light;
And men like Harvey snort with glee, and some-
    where children shout;
But there is no joy for Nick . . . or Dad . . . or
    Eastfield: The Mighty Thurman has struck out."

*Yep, you guessed her, Chester. Ol' Thurman baby went down
swinging. No one could believe it, not Dad, not Nick, not
Louis, and most of all not Thurmmy.*

*Yes-siree-bob, Nick's team lost—and in a big way. It was a
dark day for everyone. Well, almost everyone. Harvey the
Snorter seemed to be having a pretty good time. And, lucky for
me, I discovered the concession stand had a two-for-one
close-out sale. So I wasn't suffering as much as you'd expect.*

*By the way, anyone know what I can do with 247 hot dogs
and 1.3 tons of stale popcorn?*

NINE
"At the Old Ball Game"

Dad wasn't sure how long it had been since the game had ended. It could have been minutes, it could have been hours. He just didn't know.

What he did know was that the overflow crowd had now been reduced to just two concession people sweeping up; that all the cheering and clapping had been reduced to quiet rustlings of empty popcorn bags and used Pepsi cups; and what had once been the mighty coach of the mighty Braves was now just a lonely man sitting near the pitcher's mound staring at home plate. A man who felt humbled, defeated, and, yes, even a little silly.

Without a word Nick slowly approached and sat beside his father.

"How we doing?" Dad asked, still staring straight ahead.

Nick looked over his shoulder to the scoreboard, where their agonizing defeat remained etched in vivid black-and-white numbers. "Still losing," he said with a sigh.

Dad glanced at his son. There was no missing the catch in the boy's voice or the red in his eyes from crying. In an instant Dad had his arm out and was pulling Nicholas toward him.

Nick let him. To be honest, a good hug right now wasn't such a bad idea. After a moment, Dad spoke. "You know . . . I've been sitting here thinking about how bad I wanted this game. You know, beat Harvey the Snorter, manage a championship team . . . maybe conquer the world."

Nicholas tried to smile but without much luck.

"I tell you," Dad said with a sigh as he looked back to home plate, "it sure seemed like we had all the ingredients."

"Especially Thurman Miller." Nick nodded.

After another pause Dad continued. "Well, Son, I think we both found out that when you dream without the Lord . . . you'd better dream again."

Nick was already nodding. He remembered all too clearly his argument with Sarah after he'd waited on Thurman hand and foot. "Someone tried to tell me that a couple days back," he answered, "but I wouldn't—"

"You guys OK?"

The fellows looked up to see Sarah approaching. Right beside her was Mom.

"We got a little worried," Mom added. "I mean, when you didn't show at home."

Dad and Nick each gave a little shrug, almost in unison.

"Aw . . . ," Mom said. She offered her hand to help Dad stand. He took it, and once he was on his feet she gave him a reassuring hug. "How you doing, Coach?"

"Oh, a little better," Dad answered.

"You OK?" It was Sarah, and she was speaking to Nick. In fact, she was even putting her arm around him.

"Yeah," he said as he looked down a little embarrassed. In their fight he had put her down left and right. Now it was all too clear that she had just been trying to help. He knew that—now. And he knew that if he had listened to her, things might have been different. Boy, did he know it. At last he looked up at her. "Listen, I'm sorry about the other day. . . . I, uh—"

"No problem," she said, smiling.

For the first time that afternoon, Nick was also able to smile. For an older sister, Sarah wasn't bad. Not bad at all.

By now Mom had her arm around Dad and was starting to direct him back to the car. "Time to reenter the human race, sweetheart. You too, Nick."

By now both guys were feeling better. Mom was right. They had wallowed long enough in their pity party. Now it was time to get going—to get back into the game—of life.

They both knew they'd made some mistakes. Some Triple-A, megaton mistakes. Fortunately they knew the Lord—and their family—would forgive them. So it was time to get up, learn from those mistakes, and carry on.

They also knew there'd be other mistakes—some even bigger than their Thurman disaster. But that was OK, because with the Lord as their "coach," those mistakes would never become major defeats. They'd just be "golden opportunities" for learning and growing.

Of course, none of that really helped make things hurt

less. At least, not yet. But it did help everything make more sense.

Well, guys and gals, thus endeth another fun-filled, action-packed, nearly-all-expenses-paid adventure into the life and times of me and my buddy. I tell you, Nick could sure save himself a lot of trouble by asking me for advice. But I guess some things you gotta learn on your own.

Anyway, to all you jocks and jockettes out there, take care. We'll see you soon for our next exciting trip into the eerie and uncharted life of Nicky "Boy Wonder" Martin. Oh, and be sure to bring your appetites. No promises, but there still just might be a couple of these 247 hot dogs left from the game.

CHOMP-CHOMP, BURP. *Ahhhh. . . .*

Make that 246. Better hurry, they're going fast. . . .

Love your neighbor as much as you love yourself.
(Matthew 22:39; *The Living Bible*)

Beauty in the Least

by Bill Myers and Robert E. West

ONE
Things That Go Bump in the Night

"Mc-Gee, Mc-Gee, Mc-Gee . . ."

The crowd continued to chant, demanding that I, the All-American everything, once again step onto the playing field. There were just seconds left in Slobber Bowl XXXXXXXXXXXXXVII and, as usual, the day could only be saved by the magnificent and marvelously macho . . . McGee.

My team, the Anaheim Arm Pits (imagine how hard it was to find a mascot), was down by two points. One precise punt by me, their perfectly punctual punter, would clinch the championship. But after running twenty or thirty touchdowns (almost half in the right direction), kicking 23.5 field goals, and eating twice my weight in (burp) corn dogs, this poised and professionally polished punter was plainly too pooped (and plump) to punt.

"Mc-Gee, Mc-Gee, Mc-Gee . . ."

But what about my team?

What about my fans?

What about all that money I'd make selling sports shoes on TV?

Say no more. I waddled onto the field as only a wide-bodied eating machine can waddle. (Don't worry, I can shed these pounds with just a few quick strokes of an eraser. Being a pencil drawing does have a few advantages—just keep me away from those paper shredders). But I digress. Or is it digest. Hmmm, that makes me hungry—think I'll grab another corn dog for the road.

Where were we? Oh yes. I stepped onto the field. Suddenly the stadium was filled with the roar of fans, the flash of photographers, and the face of a giant outer-space monster.

A WHAT??

You guessed her, Chester. As usual, being a sports superstar was not enough for someone with my enormous ego. Now I was also being called upon to save the Earth from another invasion of outer-space giants.

I watched as the ugly creature leaned forward and stuck his giant snout down on the playing field.

Fans fled. Referees ran. Quarterbacks quaked.

But not me. No-siree-bob. I'm the hero of this story. A legend in my own mind.

The giant monster opened his giant mouth and with all of his giant fury roared, "McGEE!!!"

Suddenly the cheering fans disappeared. More suddenly still, the playing field turned into a kitchen table. Most suddenliest stiller, I was no longer holding a football, but an eraser.

Yes, once again, Nicholas Martin, my part-time creator and full-time killjoy was interrupting another one of my fabulous fantasies.

"Have you seen my eraser?" he asked as he shoved books and papers around the kitchen table.

Poor kid. As usual he was coming to me for help. And as usual I had the solution. "This what you mean, Nickster?" I quipped as I twirled the ex-football now-eraser on my finger.

"Yeah," he sighed, "I need that for this history report."

Luckily I had other ideas. "C'mon, kid, loosen up," I shouted as I tucked the eraser under my arm. "Let's make a little history of our own. A sports moment. You know . . . the thrill of victory, the agony of . . . er, well, forget that part."

Before he could argue, my marvelous imagination went into overdrive. The kitchen table became a stadium as I began to run a zigzag pattern, straight-arming everything in sight—the pencil holder, Nick's glass of milk, Mom's flower arrangement.

"He's to the thirty . . . the forty . . . midfield!" I cried doing my own play by play. "It's the run of the decade! Twelve broken tackles, five perfect reverses, and a partridge in a pear tree."

"Oh, brother," Nick groaned.

Then it happened. I got broadsided by Nick's popcorn bowl. It was a hard tackle and a lousy break, but I wasn't worried. That just meant it was time for another preeminent punt. Once again the crowd chanted my name:

"Mc-GEE, Mc-GEE, Mc-GEE . . ."

(What'd you expect them to chant? "Bugs Bunny?" "Mickey Mouse?" No way! Let those jokers find their own book series.)

Everyone waited as I prepared to punt the Pink Pearl (uh, you know, that's a brand of eraser . . . aw, never mind) to Pluto.

"But can the mighty McGee do it?" the announcer cried. "Although he is loved by every created creature . . . although he is the embodiment of everything great, noble, and, of course, humble, can he—"

"OK, McGee," Nick interrupted again. You could tell his patience was about gone. "I've got to finish this history report, so hand me the eraser."

"But there's only three seconds left," I protested. "We're two points behind. What about my team, my fans . . . what about the readers of this book? They've just waded through three pages of this football fantasy, and if there's no payoff they're really going to be ticked."

But the look on Nicky boy's face said he didn't give a rip about you . . . or me. So I quickly raced forward and kicked that eraser-ball for all I was worth (which, with the cost of paper and colored felt pens, is about $1.82).

"It's up!" I shouted. "It has the distance! It's . . . it's . . . caught by the idiot giant boy!"

Sure enough, ol' Nick caught the football and calmly went back to erasing with it.

My field became a kitchen table, and once again we were back to reality with all its boringness.

"Look," Nick sighed, "I know you're excited about our visiting Louis in Indianapolis this weekend. After all, it's our first time to see a professional football team, but if I don't get this report written, we may as well kiss those fifty-yard-line seats good-bye."

Nick pulled his paper forward and continued erasing.

"OK, keep working, Einstein," I muttered. "But how 'bout one last pass for old time's sake."

"McGee . . ."

"Please . . ."

"McGee . . ."

I could tell he was weakening. So, not having an ounce of pride in my humble body, I did what any quivering pile of pridelessness would do. I begged.

"Please-please-please-please-please-please-please . . ."

"All right . . . all right!" Nick cried.

That's all it took. In a flash I was racing across the table.

"McGee's going long!" I shouted. "He's deep! Martin's going to throw the bomb!!!"

Nick fired the eraser.

It sailed toward me.

I leaped into the air.

I caught the ball.

I looked down.

I suddenly wondered why they didn't make kitchen tables as long as they used to.

I smiled sadly to Nick. Then waved. Then dropped out of sight faster than Wile E. Coyote in a Roadrunner cartoon.

"Whoooooooaaaaa!!!"

CRASH-BOOM-TINKLE-TINKLE.

The "Whooooooaaaaa!!!" was me.

The "crash-boom" was my body hitting the floor.

And the "tinkle-tinkle?"

Got me. Though I noticed I did seem to be missing quite a few teeth.

Nick shook his head at McGee, then picked up his pencil and went back to writing. He stopped only long enough to glance at his notes and check the information in the books he had opened.

No doubt about it, Nicholas wanted to go to that Colts-Bills game with Louis. Wanted it bad. Real bad. So bad that he was willing to do just about anything—even ruin his reputation as a hater of history by getting a decent grade on his history report. That was the condition his folks made in order for him to go. Nothing like a little parental blackmail to improve the ol' GPA.

This meant Nick had been busy. So busy that he didn't

even play his standard 8½ hours of Game Boy that night. So busy that he stayed up after the rest of the family went to bed. So busy that he didn't notice a shadow as it slowly passed across the dining room window.

A SHADOW??

Hang on, there's more.

Nicholas flipped through the pages of another book, jotting down more information. Finally he'd had enough. Pro game or no pro game, he could barely keep his eyes open. It was definitely time to hit the hay. He slammed the book shut. He looked up. And—

He froze!

There it was. A shadow. Only now it was on the far wall, looming several times larger than life. After a couple of seconds of raw fear, Nick forced himself to move. Slowly he turned to look out the window and saw . . .

Nothing.

He glanced back to the wall again.

More of nothing. The shadow was gone.

He blinked, then frowned. What was going on? Nick wasn't sure, but he knew he better find out. Quietly, he slipped from the dining-room chair and crept up to the side of the window. He took a deep breath. Then, with a rush of courage, he leaped in front of the glass to face the monster head-on!

But all he faced was even more of nothing.

This was getting too weird. Nick gulped. As far as he was concerned he'd put in enough time as a superhero for one evening. Now if he could just get to the stairs, race up to his room, and dive under the covers of his bed, he'd call it a day.

The only problem was that the stairs were all the way on the other side of the room. Then there was another little matter: the knob to the back door had suddenly started to rattle!

Someone was trying to get in!

Well, it was now or never. If Nick was going to prove he was a coward he'd have to hurry and do it, before he got killed! With a spurt of speed he raced across the room, took the steps three at a time, darted into the upstairs hallway, and ran smack dab into . . .

"AUGHHHH!" Dad cried.

"AUGHHHH!" Nick answered.

They hit the ground at roughly the same time.

"What are you doing up?" Nicholas asked as he scrambled back to his feet. Then he pointed to the seven iron in Dad's hands. "And why are you carrying that golf club?"

"I thought I heard somebody in the backyard," Dad answered.

"Not anymore," Nick said. "Now they're at the back door!"

Dad winced. "Well, I guess it's up to us to save your mother and sisters," he said.

"Why couldn't I have had brothers?" Nick groaned.

Dad gave him a look. "Come on, follow me."

Reluctantly Nick obeyed as they started back toward the stairs. Carefully, step-by-step, they inched their way down.

"He was right outside," Nicholas whispered.

Dad nodded.

Once they reached the bottom of the stairs Dad

snapped off the lights. "Stay here," he whispered. "I'll go check."

Nick was more than happy to obey as his father quietly crept toward the windows.

Dad checked the first window.

Nothing.

Then the second.

Nothing again.

The third.

More nothing.

Finally he arrived at the back door. Carefully he reached for the lock and unbolted it. After a deep breath he slowly turned the nob. Then, raising his club in preparation, he quickly threw open the door to see . . .

You guessed it: even more of nothing.

He let out a low sigh of relief. "Well, whoever it was is gone now," Dad said as he lowered his golf club. He walked back to the staircase and casually flipped on the light only to be met by:

"AUGH!"

"AUGHHHHH!"

"AUGHHHHHHHHH!"

The little chorus of screams was brought to you by:

Mom holding a radio telephone . . .

Grandma toting a yardstick . . .

And Sarah wearing enough green mud on her face to scare away any burglar.

Dad broke out laughing as he surveyed all three women poised at the bottom of the stairs, ready to defend their home. "I pity anyone who tries to break into this house," he said. "But have no fear, ladies, the men are—"

A loud bang at the door made Dad finish his sentence with a yelp: *"Here!"*

In keeping with family tradition, everyone panicked. Dad dropped his seven iron and tripped over Nick, who had dropped to the floor. Mom dropped the portable phone and kept colliding with Grandma, who wrung her hands and paced in little circles.

Luckily, Sarah was safe and sound—under the kitchen table.

"What's the phone number for 9-1-1?" Mom kept crying.

Dad and Nick were too busy stumbling over each other and the golf club to answer. Finally Dad freed his club from Nick's feet just as the silhouetted figure reappeared in the window. The person began banging on the glass and shouting incoherently.

"Look, Dad!" Nicholas said, pointing. "He's holding a sign or something."

Dad rushed to the door and turned on the porch light. Suddenly the silhouette became a man. A man nearly Dad's age. The paper he held to the glass was an airline ticket folder with the name "Romanian Air."

Below this was a handwritten note. With his seven iron raised to strike, Dad moved closer. He tried to read the note, but his glasses were up in his room. Grandma's knitting basket was nearby, so he reached into it and pulled out her glasses—complete with glittering jewels and rhinestone rims. He tilted them back and forth until he was finally able to focus them on the note.

"'Michael and Ilie,'" he read. "From Romania."

"Ilie?!" Nick cried as he rushed toward the door.

"Who?" Dad asked.

The figure outside suddenly hoisted up a small boy and held him in the window for all to see, as Nick jerked open the door.

"It's Ilie Tinescu," he cried. "My pen pal from Romania!"

TWO
Untimely Visitors

Nick turned from the window where the visitors stood and shrugged sheepishly to his family. To say he was embarrassed might be an understatement. To say Nick's face was glowing like the inside of a toaster oven would be more accurate.

"Well," Dad said, returning Grandma's glasses to her basket, "I guess we should ask them in."

"I can't meet anyone looking like this!" Sarah cried, pointing to the green mud on her face. Quickly she turned and dashed back up the stairs.

Dad straightened his pajamas and walked to the open door. He was about to apologize to the guy standing there when the man's two burly arms suddenly caught him up in the world's biggest bear hug.

"Dom mnu lay, Martoni!" the huge man cried in Romanian. At least everybody guessed it was Romanian.

Dad wheezed and tried to catch his breath. Then, just about the time he was wondering if he'd have to see a chiropractor for the rest of his life, the big guy let go.

"I am Michael Tinescu," the man said in accented English, "and this is my son, Ilie."

"Hello, Meester Martin," Ilie said to Nick. "I can't

believe I finally meet you after four years!" Although the boy had his dad's broad smile, he definitely didn't have his size. In fact he was at least a foot shorter than Nick, something the pictures they'd traded hadn't shown.

"Ilie, is it really you?" Nick asked, staring at him. "You're so . . . small."

"And you are so . . . beeg!" Ilie returned cheerfully. Then, very politely, he turned to each of the other family members: "Hello, Meester Martin. Hello, Meesus Martin. Hello . . . uh . . . Grandma. Ees not correct?" he asked hesitantly.

"Very correct," Grandma answered in her usual gracious manner. "Nice to meet you, Ilie."

Ilie looked around questioningly. "But vere ees Jamie . . . and Sarah?"

"Hi, I'm Sarah." All eyes turned to see Sarah bounding down the stairs. In one brief minute she had gone from a green-faced monster to an elegantly dressed teen. "I was just looking in on Jamie," she lied. "She has a pretty bad case of the measles."

Nice save, Nick thought.

"Ahhhhh, *pooh-zah*," Ilie exclaimed. He gestured to imaginary spots on his face. "I already had *pooh-zah* . . . uh . . . measles, as you say."

"Mom's got Jamie quarantined up in her room," Sarah added. She looked down at Ilie then glanced over at Nick as if to say, *Isn't he a little small to be your pen pal?*

Nick just gave her a look back that said, *Why don't you go back to your swamp!*

(Isn't brother-sister communication amazing?)

"Sarah," Michael interrupted with great emotion. "Caring for your seester when she has the measles . . . true American kindness."

Sarah nodded in embarrassment. She wasn't crazy about lying, but how do you tell a foreigner that you were wearing green mud all over your face? And how do you explain that if you had greeted them in it, they'd have been halfway back across the Atlantic by now—without a boat?

"Ah, excuse the way the rest of us are dressed," Mom spoke up. She pulled her robe about her and stepped up to Michael. "But Nick wasn't expecting Ilie until Lent, so—"

"Lent? *Ja*, of course, ve're right on time," Michael said, shaking her hand. "Today ees first day of our Christmas Lenten season. The relief organization I vork for send me and Ilie to USA, to big meeting in Meessh-ee-gun."

Michael's English wasn't the best, and it took a little effort to figure out what he said as he continued. "But if we are inquisition . . ." (chances are he meant "imposition"). He turned and motioned his son toward the door. "Come, Ilie, upon these nice people we must not untrude." (Chances are he meant "intrude.")

Either way you say it, the Martins realized a major mistake had been made about the dates of Ilie's visit, and now the two Romanians were about to leave.

Nick hurried forward. "No, no, you aren't . . . 'untruding.'" He turned to his mother. "Are they, Mom?"

Of course, they'd all been expecting Ilie's visit. Sure, they'd thought it was happening in about another six months, but it wasn't Michael and Ilie's fault that

89

Romanians celebrate Lent at a different time of year than Americans.

"Why, no. Of course not," Mom exclaimed, trying to sound sincere. "Please stay," she insisted. Suddenly she noticed Dad still clutching his golf club. "Uh, David," she murmured, giving him an elbow.

Dad looked down and saw the club in his hand. He quickly grinned. "Oh! . . . uh . . . just practicing," he said, giving the club a few twists of the wrist. Then he awkwardly set it aside and asked, "Can we help you with your bags?"

"No, ve have only zees one," Michael answered.

"Only one bag?" Mom asked.

"Romania, she ess not a rich country," Michael explained. "Much vee do not have."

"Oh," Dad said a little embarrassed. "Well, listen, come on and follow me upstairs. Sarah, you can move in with Grandma for the night. And Nick, if you'll get the cot from the basement, Ilie can stay in your room."

Ilie whooped out something in Romanian.

"Uh . . . right. Sure," Nick answered, not having a clue what the boy had said.

As Dad led Michael and Ilie up the stairs, Mom called to them, "Can I get you anything to eat?"

"No thank you, Meesus Martin," Michael called back down. "Ve have late dinner."

Just before they disappeared, Michael turned to his son and spoke in Romanian again, *"Iubeste vecinul t'au."*

Nick stood near the kitchen table and gave a shrug. Once again he hadn't a clue about what was just said.

Fortunately ol' Nicky boy had left my sketchpad on the table, so I'd heard the whole thing. Yeah, it's me, the marvelous McGee again, and all I had to say was . . .

Romanians, my foot.

"Hey, Nick," I whispered. "Did you hear that secret code! They look like Soviet agents to me."

Nick rolled his eyes. "They were speaking Romanian, McGee. Besides, there are no more Soviet agents," he whispered, glancing up toward the staircase.

"Don't tell me you buy that whole collapse of the Soviet Union thing," I scorned. "Pure propaganda."

Suddenly there was a loud buzzer. Obviously the timing device to some bomb that was about to go off. So being the world-renowned and courageous secret agent I am, I did what any world-renowned and courageous secret agent would do . . . I leaped back into the sketchpad and hid for my life.

Nick did a little leaping too . . . until he noticed the buzzing came from an intercom he had rigged up for Jamie on the kitchen counter. He sighed and shook his head. After tonight he wondered if his nerves were ever going to be the same.

"This is Jamie," a voice said from the speaker. "Can you bring me some ginger ale? . . . and a graham cracker?"

Nick groaned and crossed over to the contraption. He pushed the button above the speaker. "Plain or cinnamon?" he asked.

"Uh . . . one of each," the voice answered.

Nick headed for the cupboard wondering if making the intercom for his sick sister had been such a good idea after all.

A few minutes later Nicholas was in his bedroom arm wrestling with an old army cot. The legs were going every which way except down.

Meanwhile, Ilie was taking in the sights of Nick's room like it was Disneyland. "Eet ees just as I imagined from your letters! You are so lucky to live een such a place."

Suddenly he noticed Nick's computer screen. On it was a sketch of McGee. "Ahhh, a computer with your McGee drawing!" He crossed to it, staring wide-eyed. "Amazink!"

"Yeah, that's kinda new," Nick said as he continued to fight the legs of the cot.

"Eet ees so amazink," Ilie went on as he reached out to touch a button on the side. "Vat do zese button do?"

He soon had his answer. The screen completely blanked out. He had turned off the computer.

Nick looked up, his face draining of color. "Uh . . . no problem," he said with a gulp. "I just wish I'd saved it first."

Continuing his tour of the room, Ilie noticed a bright red model glider bracketed to the wall above Nick's bed. "Zees ees vonderful, Nick. . . . Zees must be ze model plane you wrote about!" He took his shoes off and stood on the bed, shifting the glider about for a better look.

Suddenly very protective of his things, Nick tried the old distraction routine. "Uhhh . . . did you ever finish the model you wrote about—you know, that ship with the Romanian name?"

"The *Carpaithia?*" Ilie asked, turning away from the glider. "I finished eet, but I no longer have eet," he said as he stepped off the bed. "I needed ze wood for anozer project, so . . ."

As Ilie talked, Nick edged over to the bed and read-justed the glider. It wouldn't do for things to get out of kilter just because somebody dropped in for a visit.

Next, Ilie noticed Nicholas's Game Boy. Nick immediately stiffened with fear as the kid picked it up. He wanted to yank it out of Ilie's hands, but somehow he figured that wouldn't exactly help international relations.

Luckily, Ilie was suddenly distracted by Nick's skate-board. Before Nick had time to protest, Ilie had hopped on it and started zipping across the room toward the art table. "I see zees in movie—*Back to zee Future*," he exclaimed.

Unfortunately, nobody in the movie had said anything about how to stop! Nick dove for him and swung him off just as the board sailed under the table.

"Uh . . . thanks, Neeck," Ilie said with a nervous laugh. "I could use a leetle practice, maybe in a much beeger place."

"Right." Nick nodded. His nerves on edge, he returned to fixing the impossible-to-fix cot. "Hey," he said, trying to change the subject, "what was that your dad said to you in Romanian just before you came up the stairs?"

Ilie reached into his duffel bag and pulled out a Romanian Bible. "Eet ees from Matthew twenty-two," he said as he thumbed through the pages. "You must know zees one, Nick. *'Iubeste vecinul t'au iubeste vencinu.'*"

"Uh . . . ," Nick hedged, "mine must be a different translation."

"Ah," Ilie laughed, "een English eet means you must love your neighbor as much as you love yourself."

"Oh, sure," Nicholas agreed. "I know that one."

Ilie nodded in satisfaction and turned back to rummage in his duffel bag. Nick craned his neck for a better look. He wondered what foreign and exotic things Ilie had stashed inside. Finally with great flourish the boy pulled out—

"A toothbrush?" Nicholas asked in surprise.

"Yes." Ilie agreed with a grin. "My very own. Now, could you tell me vhere ees zee . . . zee—" He couldn't seem to find the word.

"The bathroom?" Nick volunteered.

"Yes . . . yes . . . zee bassroom," Ilie repeated.

"Down the hall," Nick said, trying not to laugh. "First door on the right."

Ilie closed his bag and started for the door. Then he turned with an even bigger grin. "I can't believe vee get to stay here a whole veek!" With that he headed back down the hall.

Nick stared after him. "A week!" he gasped. What about Louis? What about the Colts-Bills game?! He couldn't just leave Ilie here while he took off for Indianapolis. Could he?

Suddenly things weren't turning out so well. In fact, they were turning out pretty awful. Sure, Nick had been excited about meeting Ilie . . . but talk about lousy timing!

In disgust he plopped down on the cot, which immediately collapsed under his weight.

THREE
Busy Bodies

RIIIING!

Mom ignored the doorbell and continued working in the kitchen.

RIIIING!

More ignoring. More working.

RIIIING!

Even more ignoring. Even more . . . well, you probably get the picture. The reason was simple. The doorbell had been ringing all morning. And by "all morning" we're not just talking all morning; we're talking *ALL MORNING*.

You see, Michael had volunteered to fix it. And fixing it meant ringing it. Unfortunately, the ringing bell was on the kitchen wall right above where Mom was working . . . which probably explains why she was getting "rung out."

"I've got to make something for their dinner," she muttered while thumbing through a cookbook. "Ahh, what's this? . . . 'Romanian Cabbage Casserole' . . ." She read on, "Hollow a large summer squash. Add six heads of green cabbage and steam 'til limp."

RIIIING!

Mom jumped for the hundredth time. But this was a "new and improved" jump. This time she dropped the book, which hit the rolling pin, which crashed into a tomato, which rolled off the counter nearly becoming pizza sauce . . . until Mom made one of her famous catches.

"That doorbell is driving me nuts!" she cried.

Now, as we all know, Mom's pretty cool under pressure. But with Thanksgiving coming up, instant house guests, a little girl with measles, and nonstop ringing bells . . . well, she was definitely showing signs of thermonuclear meltdown.

Then, just as Michael walked in, Jamie's intercom suddenly buzzed. "Not to vorry," Michael said cheerfully, "I am almost finished." He began adjusting the bell above her.

"Just a minute, honey," Mom called into the intercom.

Michael looked at her nervously. He'd heard of American friendliness, but calling near strangers "honey" seemed a bit much. Before the woman could hit him with a "sweetheart" or a "darling," he changed the subject.

"Back home," he said, "one press of the finger produces long, steady, forceful ring. Ven I am through, yours vill do same!"

"Michael," Mom said, smiling weakly, "I know the bell has been on David's fix-it list for a while, and . . . uh, thank you for repairing it and all, but—"

"My pleasure!" Michael chimed in. "Zis way, when guests come, zey don't need to go to back door and scare family as we did last night!"

Mom sighed as Michael headed for the front door again. She wasn't sure what he meant by the phrase "long, forceful ring," but—

RIIIIIIIIIIIIIIIIIIIIIIIIIIIIIIINNNNNGGGG!

She was getting the idea.

As the sound of the doorbell slowly faded, Ilie skipped down the stairs and into the kitchen. "Good morning, Meesus Martin. Look what I made you." He handed her a large, wooden, hand-carved something-or-other.

Mom was at a loss for words. It was big and intricately carved, but a big and intricately carved *what*? "Uh . . . thank you," she finally said, carefully looking it over for clues.

At last she noticed the safety pin on the back. *A pin,* she thought. *But it's so big. . . .*

"You're velcome," Ilie beamed as he stood waiting for her to pin it onto her blouse.

Reluctantly, Mom unlatched the pin and stuck it on. "There," she said forcing her best smile.

"Uh, Meesus Martin," Ilie hesitated, "you've . . . peenned eet upside down."

"Oh, sorry," Mom said in embarrassment as she fumbled to turn it around. "I knew that." At last she pinned it correctly.

Ilie broke into another grin and strolled out of the kitchen with the look of satisfaction spread across his face.

RIIIIIIIIIIIIIIIIIIIIIIIIIIIIIIINNNNNNNNG!

Mom gave another jump—not only at the ring but at the sight of Nick half-falling, half-stumbling down the stairs. "Will someone answer that door?" he grumbled, still asleep.

Mom sighed.

Nicholas lumbered over to the breakfast table and

slung his backpack onto the chair. It was about then he noticed Mom's pin. "I see the Romanian wood fiend has struck again," he moaned.

"He made you a gift, too?" Mom asked.

Nicholas unzipped his backpack and pulled out a beautifully carved wooden cup. "I think it's supposed to be a pencil holder," he grumbled. "Who knows."

Mom raised an eyebrow at his tone. "Sounds like someone got up on the wrong side of the cot."

"There is no *right* side to that cot," he mumbled as he poured himself some orange juice. "Even when I stay over at Louis's, his bunk bed isn't that hard."

"Oh, that reminds me," Mom said, "you'd better call Louis and tell him you can't go to the game."

"But Mom!" Nick cried, suddenly wide awake. "This will be the first pro game I see!"

"I'm sorry," Mom said, shaking her head, "but you're Ilie's host. You can't just get up and leave in the middle of his visit. Louis will understand."

Nick was furious. Sleeping on the cot was bad enough, but missing his first pro game because Ilie was visiting . . . well, that was definitely pushing the meaning of "hospitality."

Mom read his thoughts perfectly. "We all have to make sacrifices, dear."

"But why am *I* always the one?" Nick whined.

"I don't think you're the only one," Mom complained. "Thanksgiving dinner is tough enough with your sister sick." She opened the cupboard and began looking for some cans. "But toss in a few last-minute guests, ringing bells, and some Romanian cabbage casserole and—"

Suddenly Ilie and Michael entered the room together.

"Ze bell . . . she ees fixed," Michael announced proudly. He reached up and replaced the box back over the bell. "Next I fix faulty light."

He crossed to the wall switch next to the sink. "Most perplexing. When you turn on switch, instead of light," he flipped on the switch, "out comes terrible rumble from sink."

There was a rumble all right—from the garbage disposal!

"It's all right, Michael," Mom said as she hurried over to turn off the disposal. "It's supposed to do that."

Once again the intercom buzzer sounded.

"Ees someone at ze door?" Michael asked, puzzled that his doorbell was now making a buzzing noise.

"No, that's Jamie," Mom sighed, as she crossed to the intercom.

"Mom," Jamie's voice crackled from the speaker, "you forgot to bring me a spoon for my cereal."

"Sorry . . ."

Jamie continued. "And every time the doorbell rings there's static on the TV."

Michael stooped down to examine the little speaker. "This ees amazing device," he exclaimed.

"Yeah, it keeps me busy," Mom agreed.

"Did we get chocolate milk yet?" Jamie's voice asked.

"Uh . . . sorry, sweetie," Mom said. "I forgot."

Michael's smile broadened. "Ilie and me go to store for you! All our lives have we heard tales of American gro-sir-ee stores like we see on TV een *You Love Lucy.* Fred, Ethel, Lucy, and Rickie go to store and—"

"Well, great," Mom interrupted, trying to hide her impatience. She crossed to her purse and pulled out her billfold. "And get some more cabbage, too. Nick can show you how to get there on his way to school."

"But Mom," Nick whined . . . until he saw her no-nonsense look. You know the one. The one your parents use that says, "You can argue with me on some things, but you WILL OBEY me on this one."

Nick sighed. "Sure," he said with a forced shrug, "it's on the way."

Mom started to hand Michael a ten-dollar bill. But he lifted his hand and refused. In Romanian he said, *"Omul ejte ch un porc care nu se mai auce vnapoi unde a locuit."*

Ilie saw the puzzled looks on Mom's and Nick's faces, so he translated for his dad. "Zat ees old Romanian saying: A man ees a swine who denies bacon to his neighbor."

Mom gave a weak, "Thank you," then turned and exchanged "Hoo-boy!" looks with Nick.

This was definitely going to be *some* Thanksgiving.

The walk to town wasn't bad. It wasn't great, either.

Try as he might to stay cool, Nick found himself getting a little frustrated with Michael and Ilie. They were constantly stopping and staring at this or pointing at that. It was like they were visiting from another planet.

Then there was their friendliness. I mean, did they have to greet *everybody* they saw?

When they passed a house covered with Thanksgiving decorations, both Michael and Ilie burst out laughing. Nick didn't see what was so funny. (He would never have guessed it had anything to do with the funny Pilgrims in funny clothes and funny Pilgrim hats, pointing funny rifles at turkeys.)

Then there was the school-crossing guard. Everything was going fine until Michael and Ilie stood at attention and saluted the guy. Nick rolled his eyes and prodded them on across, shrugging sheepishly to the guard.

It seemed the more time they spent together, the more distant Nick felt from Ilie. They'd been closer when they were five thousand miles apart. Now that the guy was here, in person, Nick felt like a tour guide for extraterrestrials. Weird. A friend from halfway around the world comes to visit, and suddenly all kinds of things bug you—like the way he looks and talks and walks. OK, like everything.

Finally they reached the business district. Michael and Ilie were totally blown away. They turned around in a circle, slowly taking it all in: hardware stores, clothing stores, shoe stores, food stores, and window displays showing everything from vacuum cleaners to computers, tomatoes to toasters, Reeboks to ripsaws.

Nick glanced at his watch. "Well, this is where we split up," he said gratefully. "The grocery store is about a block that away." He turned and pointed up the street. "You can't miss it. I get back from school around two so we can—"

But when he turned back to them, they were gone.

"What on earth . . ."

Then he spotted them. They were walking down the alley toward a trash dumpster. He started after them.

"Guys!" he shouted. "Guys, don't go in there. That's the wrong way!"

Soon it was Nick who felt like an extraterrestrial—like he was the one visiting another world. Back alleys were one place he never went. But, with a deep breath for courage, he stepped in.

Deep, menacing shadows seemed to loom from all sides. Dark, grimy walls towered high above him. Graffiti was everywhere. His foot slipped on a pile of trash, and when he reached down to stop himself from falling, he came up with something slimy and smelly on his hand. A dozen flies swarmed around it. And, of course, there was the smell.

At last he reached Michael and Ilie. They were at the dumpster. The dumpster where a large figure slowly rose from inside. The figure of a huge, menacing man in rags. A man known throughout the city.

Crazy Jim!

FOUR
Another World

"Uh . . . hello!" Michael said. He extended his hand to Crazy Jim like they were next-door buddies. "I am Michael Tinescu and zis ees my son—"

Suddenly he stopped. He realized Crazy Jim was standing in the middle of a garbage dumpster and figured it might be a good idea to help him out. "Oh, let me assist you. . . ."

"Please," Crazy Jim said in his best British accent. "Watch the cuffs."

Nick tugged anxiously at Michael's arm and whispered, "That's Crazy Jim! He's a bum and—"

"A bump?" Michael asked.

Before Nicholas could answer, Crazy Jim suddenly leaped out of the dumpster. "I prefer the term 'gentleman of reduced means,'" he said as he politely tipped his hat. "James Tilman the Third at your service."

"Sorry Crazy . . . I mean James," Nicholas stuttered. He glanced nervously around. This was not the place he wanted to be. Nor was Crazy Jim a man he wanted to be there with. "We were just, uh . . . we were just leaving."

Nick quickly turned, but Crazy Jim darted in front of him. "A word to the wise," he said as he blocked Nick's way with a battered umbrella. "When escorting out-of-towners about, one would do well to advise them to keep their hands to themselves."

Nick gave a nervous laugh.

But Michael paid no attention. He just resumed babbling to Crazy Jim like they were old friends. "I am worker in relief organization," he said, pulling out his wallet. "But before, I was steel worker in Brasnov."

"Brasnov?" Crazy Jim asked seriously. "Is that near Akron?"

Michael laughed at what he thought was a joke and slapped Crazy Jim on the back. He pulled out a worn photo from his wallet and showed it to him. "Here ees wife at volunteer aid station, following beeg earthquake. And see, here ees son, Ilie—" he pointed to another picture, then turned to Ilie—"who ees here vis me now."

Crazy Jim looked at the boy, but Michael still wasn't finished. "Tell me," he asked, turning to Nick, "what ees meaning of word, *crazy*?"

Crazy Jim jumped in to explain. "Uh . . . I prefer the Old English definition," he said, smiling. . . . "'Crazy: possessing enthusiasm or excitement.'"

"Ah, yes," Michael said, suddenly nodding in understanding, "like me!"

Nick could only cough slightly. And then, right on cue, he saw Jordan Michaels, his athletic buddy, standing at the entrance to the alley.

"Hey, Nick? Is that you?" Jordan yelled as he started to approach. "What are you doing down here?"

"Jordan." Nick pretended to smile. This wasn't exactly the type of occasion you'd invite your friends to, but he decided to make the best of it. "Uh, Jordan . . . this is my friend Ilie Tinescu and his dad, Michael . . . they're from Romania."

"Hello!" Michael answered in his usual enthusiasm. Then, turning to Crazy Jim, he continued, "Zis is my friend, James!"

"A pleasure to make your acquaintance, Master Jordan," Crazy Jim said, again politely tipping his hat.

"Yeah, uh . . . hi," Jordan stammered, completely confused. "Uh, listen Nick, if we don't hurry we're gonna be late for school."

"That's right," Nick said a little too agreeably. "We'd better get going."

"Of course," Michael nodded.

"Good-bye," Ilie added.

"Au revoir." Crazy Jim grinned.

Nick gave a nod, turned, and hurried out of the alley with his friend.

"I can't believe this, Jordan," he whispered. "First, I find out I have to miss a trip to the Colts-Bills game because of these guys, and now I'm on a first-name basis with Crazy Jim! What am I going to do?"

"Hey," Jordan cracked, "maybe Crazy Jim will put them up for you so you can go to the game."

"Very funny!" Nicholas sighed, "very funny." Then, just before they rounded the corner he turned back to the three of them. "Don't forget!" he yelled. "The grocery store is two blocks down the street."

"Ve understand," Michael called as he threw his arm around Crazy Jim.

"Bye, Neeck," Ilie called. "Ve'll see you at home. America ees really amazink!!"

"Yeah," Nick murmured as he turned and walked down the street. All he could think was that this wasn't the America he knew. *Normal* people—*good* people—didn't live in alleys and go through dumpsters. He wasn't exactly sure where it said that in the Bible, but he figured it must be there someplace.

What he didn't know was that his figuring would change.

Soon.

Very soon.

If Nick had looked down the alley in the other direction, he'd have noticed someone else rummaging through trash cans. But this someone else was no Crazy Jim. Oh, he was dressed almost as poorly as Crazy Jim, and he was sifting through the garbage as carefully as Crazy Jim. But this someone was only ten years old.

His name was Steven.

"All right!" Steven cried as he pulled half a potato out of a can. He checked it over for spoiled spots, then wiped it clean and stuffed it into his sweatshirt pocket next to a scrawny bunch of carrots that were sticking out.

He crossed to another set of trash cans. He opened the first one but immediately slammed it shut again. The smell was just too awful.

The second can was filled mostly with paper. He was about to close it when something caught his eye. He reached inside and came up with a football card.

"Hey!" he cheered, holding one up high. "It's Jim Kelly!"

He rummaged around for more and finally came up with four others. He carefully wiped them off and started to stuff them into his frayed back pocket when he suddenly heard a voice.

"Well, whaddaya know!"

Steven whirled around. Four boys stood there, all neatly dressed in the latest jeans and coats. They stood blocking the alley—and any chance Steven had to make a run for it.

Steven didn't know any of them personally, but by the smirk on their faces he recognized their species: *Genus Bullicus.*

Better known as "bullies."

For a ten-year-old, Steven could handle himself pretty well. Since his family had lost their house three months ago, he'd learned fast—he'd had to—but there were four of these guys and only one of him. And they were bigger. A lot bigger. Mostly eighth graders, he guessed.

Steven stuffed the last football card into his back pocket and tried to walk past the boys, but they would have none of it.

"A real fashion statement, ain't he," a tall skinny one said as he stepped in front of Steven.

"Yeah, nice threads," another said as he flicked a torn fragment of Steven's sleeve.

"It's the latest thing," the biggest and ugliest said as he grabbed Steven's back pocket and easily ripped it down. "It comes apart in your hand."

Everyone laughed as the football cards fluttered to the ground.

"Come on!" Steven protested, as he bent down to scoop them up.

But the big guy's foot suddenly appeared on top of them. He ground his heel into them and growled, "We don't want you freaks cluttering up our streets. You ruin the neighborhood!"

"We do not!" Steven argued, tugging at the big guy's leg, trying to pull the cards free. "We got as much right here as—"

"You got nothin'!" the big guy shouted as he quickly lifted his foot and kicked Steven. The little guy went rolling and crashing into another set of cans as the rest of the boys broke out laughing.

"You don't got rights, man," the big guy sneered. "'Cause you're garbage. Just more garbage cluttering up our streets."

"That's right," the tall, skinny kid nodded as the group started for Steven again. "My old man says you bums bring property value down and ruin business."

"Yeah," the others agreed.

"That's right," the big guy grumbled. "So you better get outta here."

Steven hesitated.

"GET OUT OF HERE!"

Steven needed no more invitations. Without a word, he jumped to his feet and raced down the alley for all he was worth—but even while he ran there was no missing the tears as they streaked down his dirty cheeks.

FIVE
Sour Grapes

It was cold Wednesday morning. Cold enough to make everybody look like steam engines as they walked downtown blowing out little puffs of white breath. But Dad, who was nice and warm in his car, barely noticed those walking by as he squealed around the corner and drove into his parking spot at the newspaper.

He was late. In fact he'd been late every day that week. He wasn't sure, but he thought it had something to do with Ilie and Michael. With the way they loved to talk before breakfast . . . during breakfast . . . after breakfast . . . and anytime in between.

Dad raced from his car toward the building. His overcoat tails billowed behind him like wings. Halfway to the revolving doors, he screeched to a halt. He whirled around, ran back to his car, grabbed his briefcase, and started all over again.

He almost made it to the doors when Crazy Jim suddenly stepped out.

"Greetings, my good man," Jim said cheerfully. He held out his hat like it was a church collection plate. "May I impose upon you to lighten the burden of one whose misfortune it has been to—"

He stopped as Dad fumbled in his pocket and pulled out a wad of dollar bills and some change.

Crazy Jim's eyes grew big at the sight of the dollars. They grew small at the sight of the single quarter Dad dropped into his hat.

"Genuine coin of the realm," Crazy Jim muttered sarcastically. "Hope it doesn't set ya back." He tipped his hat as Dad moved through the door.

For a brief moment Dad felt guilty, but he quickly dismissed the feeling. After all, he was a busy man with lots of things to do.

Crazy Jim stretched, took a deep breath, and started walking. With his feet on automatic pilot, he slowly made his way into a nearby alley. Before he knew it he was standing underneath a large cross. Below it was a sign that read, "Back Alley Mission and Soup Kitchen."

The mission was always good for a fair breakfast, but today there was an extra little attraction. Besides the usual collection of tattered people standing in front of the door, there was a father and son playing a mandolin and singing Romanian folk songs. A father and son who looked exactly like Michael and Ilie.

And with good reason. They *were* Michael and Ilie!

Actually Michael was the one doing the singing and playing. Ilie was passing around a pink bakery box full of pastries and donuts. It wasn't the lowest calorie breakfast these homeless folks had ever had, but who was counting calories? Not these guys. By the looks of things it had been a long time since they had to worry about having too much to eat.

Back at the Martin house things were getting pretty hectic. By afternoon, the kitchen looked like a food factory. Grandma was peeling yams, and Mom was spending more time with cabbage than she had ever dreamed possible.

Ilie, who had finally left the mission, was now pursuing a brand-new project. He charged into the kitchen shouting excitedly, "My friends, I vant you all to meet Julia!"

A nice-looking girl in her twenties appeared in the doorway.

Mom pushed a stray curl out of her eyes and looked up. With the room dripping in steam from the bubbling foods and her hands dripping with cabbage juice, it was not a good time for meeting new people. But this new person was a little different. She wore a uniform—a mail carrier's uniform.

"Julia has been bringing letters and packages to zis house for months," Ilie continued, "but she has *never met ze people inside!* Can you believe eet?"

"Oh really?" Mom said, trying to sound surprised.

Actually, it wasn't all that surprising. People live in houses. Mail carriers bring them mail. No biggie. Sure, they might nod at each other in passing, but they don't usually sit down and have tea together—not unless they live in old *Andy Griffith Show* reruns. It wasn't anything personal, it was just the way things tended to be in our fast-paced society.

It was clear Julia was feeling a little awkward about the situation. She fidgeted and cleared her throat. "Uh, I usually don't, you know, meet a lot of the people on my route, but Ilie here was so insistent that—"

"She vas telling me about your Thanksgiving holiday!" Ilie interrupted. "It's amazink!"

"Oh? Do you have big plans?" Grandma asked Julia.

"Not really." Julia shrugged. "My roommate and I will probably cook up a bird in the microwave and watch reruns of the parade on TV."

"How . . . lovely," Grandma answered a little uncertainly. "I guess Thanksgiving isn't quite the event it used to be." She wiped her hands and came out from behind the counter. "When I was a child my mother used to have the whole family over . . . and neighbors, too."

Grandma sat on a stool, smiling. "You've never seen so much food: turkey and stuffing, potatoes and gravy, fresh biscuits . . ." Her voice sadly trailed off.

"That sounds really nice," Julia said, trying to picture it.

"Suddenly I am hungry!" Ilie laughed.

Mom smiled as she returned to her Romanian cabbage casserole. "Thanksgiving is more than just a big family meal," she said to Ilie. "It's a celebration of the time our forefathers gave thanks to God for all he had given them. It's a time of sharing your own good fortune with others."

For a moment it sounded like Mom was giving a sermon. But, even as the words came out of her mouth, she was thinking things like, *I wish all these people would leave so I could get back to work*, and, *These holidays are killing me*, and, *Where did I put that soup strainer?*

So much for "sharing your own good fortune with others." You see, like Nicholas, Mom had forgotten a little bit about the spirit of Thanksgiving.

After another awkward moment of silence Julia shifted

her mailbag and said, "Well, it's been nice meeting you, but I'd better be getting back to my route."

"Nice meeting you, Julia," Grandma said, still smiling.

Mom, however, was too busy with her work to smile. "Ilie, would you please show Julia out?" she asked as she stuck her head into the cupboard.

"Yes, I would!" Ilie answered brightly. "Come, Julia!" he said as he grabbed her hand and practically yanked her toward the door.

Suddenly, the new intercom buzzed.

"Mom," Jamie's voice whined, "Whatever ate my crackers!"

"Now it's the *dog*," Mom sighed. "I'm not going to make it." She wearily plopped down a box of bread crumbs on the counter and reached for the button.

Ya think ol' Mom was in a bad mood, you should've been around when Nicky boy came home from school. Then again, maybe you shouldn't have. Then again, maybe I shouldn't have. 'Course, I don't have much choice in the matter. As an imaginary character, I kinda have to go wherever Nick's imagination goes. It's in my contract.

Anyway, Nick knew this was the day he'd have to call Louis and cancel going to that football game. The kid was definitely bummed . . . big time.

But not me. No-siree-bob. I was up on his drawing table building my world-famous "Spy-Tracking Globule"—the preferred globule of spy trackers everywhere. (Don't ask me why we call it a "globule." Probably 'cause it looks like a wad of bubble gum with wires sticking out every which way. But there

113

was a good reason it looked like that. It WAS a wad of bubble gum with wires sticking out every which way.)

Anyhoo, I still didn't buy the idea that Michael and his boy blunder were do-gooders who'd come to America to help. Who did they think they were kidding? I know top-secret Soviet spies when I see them. And this Spy-Tracking Globule would help me see them . . . anywhere . . . day or night.

I continued my last-minute adjustments on the marvelous maze of merchandise as Nick dialed up Indianapolis and began his little "Whine Time" with Louis. "I've tried everything," he moaned into the phone, "but I'm stuck here, baby-sitting my friend from Romania and his fath—"

That's all I remember. Suddenly my incredibly intuitive inventive invention ignited. (Translation for you younger readers: It blowed up and goed big boom.)

The room was filled with more smoke than the boy's lavatory at lunchtime. I was fried faster than a fly in a bug zapper.

And the Spy-Tracking Globule? Rumor has it, it was raining bubble gum as far away as Toledo.

It was back to the drawing board . . . literally.

As McGee went back to work, Nick remained on the phone complaining to Louis.

"I mean, Ilie and I just don't have anything in common." He plopped down on his bed with the phone stuck to his ear and continued. "His idea of fun is hanging out with street people. And you wouldn't believe what he just brought home—our mail girl!"

Nick toyed with the wooden cup Ilie had made him as he grumbled on. "He was OK as a pen pal, but he's just too much of a Dweeb-O-Matic to be in the same country with." He took aim at the trash can and tossed the cup across the room.

Nicholas didn't pay much attention to the cup after it left his hand.

Someone else, however, noticed the cup right away. Ilie had just come down the hall and was about to enter Nick's room when he saw the cup bounce off the trash can and roll across the floor.

Then he heard Nick's voice: "I just wish Ilie and his dad had never come."

Ilie's nonstop smile suddenly stopped. He tried to swallow back the lump that quickly formed in his throat, but it did no good. Then there was the burning in his eyes. He did his best to blink back the tears, but with little success. Finally he turned and headed back down the hall toward the stairs.

A couple of seconds later Nick finished his conversation with Louis. He hung up with the world's longest sigh just as Mom whisked in. She looked even more frayed than before as she carried a tray of dirty dishes from Jamie's room.

"Do you have Jamie's Walkman?" she asked.

"Yeah," Nicholas said. "Ilie was using it over by the art table." Then, making sure his voice dripped with sarcasm, he continued, "It was, of course, amazink."

Mom turned to him. "What's wrong with Ilie, anyway?" she asked.

"Do you want the long list or the short list?" Nick muttered as he plopped back down on his bed.

"No, I mean now," Mom said as she glanced toward the door. "He looked pretty upset. I just passed him outside your door, and he didn't say a word."

A look of panic flashed across Nick's face. He lurched up from his bed. *What?!* In a flash he was off the bed and rushing to look up and down the hallway.

Ilie was nowhere in sight.

Seconds later Nick was tumbling down the staircase and into the family room . . . just as Sarah entered through the door.

"Sarah," he cried, grabbing her by the shoulders. "Have you seen Ilie?!"

"Well, yeah," she said, looking a little startled. "He and his dad just left."

"What?!" Nick yelped. He turned and raced for the door.

"I was coming in," Sarah continued, "and they left. Funny thing is, they were carrying their suitcase."

Nick barely heard her as he flung open the screen door and raced outside. But neither Ilie nor Michael were in view.

A sick feeling welled up in Nick's stomach. He was sure now that Ilie had heard his conversation with Louis.

And he knew the boy and his father were leaving. . . .

And he knew whose fault it was.

SIX
Missing Persons

Nicky boy had really blown it. Big time. And, as usual, it was up to me to unblow it—bigger time. Yes-siree-bob, somebody had to find Ilie and Michael. Somebody with brains, humility, and good looks—and let's not forget the great hair—but in addition to all those amazingly awesome attributes, it had to be somebody with a new and improved . . . Spy-Tracking Globule.

That's right. My little gizmo was finally up and working. Already it had answers to such questions as, How come kids can chew gum at home but not at school? Why do Moms hate to see their sons lying around the house when there are leaves to rake? And, most important, Why do cats always use their litter box just as soon as you've cleaned it?

But that was small potatoes compared to the real question at hand: Where were Ilie and Michael?

At the moment, I was hidden away in my handy-dandy traveling spy laboratory—better known as Nick's coat pocket. Here I dialed dials, switched switches, and knobbed knobs.

Suddenly I heard it:

Beep-beep-beep-(burp) . . .

The beeps were my machine locking onto its target. (The burp was one too many cans of Diet Dr. Pepper.)

Nicholas opened his coat pocket, looked inside, and, in his best whine, complained, "McGee, this is never going to work. We'll never find Ilie and his dad."

"What are you talking about?" I cried. "Can't you hear the beeping? The Tracking Globule glob that I stuck on their suitcase is sending out the signal!"

"McGee . . ."

I guess the kid was a little doubtful about the machine's accuracy. So far we'd tracked down a giant bank building, an '84 Oldsmobile, and . . . a fire hydrant.

Amazing! What a device! What an inventor! Who else could have found such objects? . . . I mean, I'll bet no one even knew they were missing in the first place! Now, if that's not genius, I'd like to know what is.

"C'mon, trust me," I insisted, "we'll find them in no time." Suddenly the beeps grew louder.

"See? What'd I tell you!" I shouted. "We got 'em! They're just around that corner! Hurry!"

Reluctantly Nick started to run. We reached the corner, raced around it, and ran smack-dab into . . .

WHOOOOAAAA . . . CRASH!

. . . Julia, the mail lady.

We knocked that babe flatter than a football playing chicken with a semi. There were more stars circling her head than Academy Award night in Hollywood.

Nick and I were also on the ground. He was a little dazed, but not me. One of the nice things about being a cartoon character is that when you get flattened, you always pop back up as good as new for the next scene.

Nick scrambled to his feet. Julia, however, wasn't quite so fast. In fact, she was still lying on the sidewalk stretched out in

*a thick pool of . . . a thick pool of . . . ENVELOPES! (AHA!
You thought I was going to say blood, didn't you? I tell ya,
you've got to stop watching all that violence on TV. In fact, I
know this great video series about a kid with an imaginary cartoon friend who is incredibly handsome and . . . well, never
mind, we'll talk about that some other time.)*

Immediately Nicholas was offering Julia his hand. "Sorry
about that," he said with more than a little embarrassment.

"That's OK," she said, with more than a little wobbling.
"Occupational hazard."

"You haven't by any chance seen Ilie have you?" Nick asked
as he helped her pick up the scattered envelopes. "You know,
the boy who—"

"How could I forget?" Julia chuckled as she swung her bag
across her shoulder. "Thanks to him I'm on a first-name basis
with everyone in the neighborhood, including their cats and
dogs."

Nicholas tried to laugh. *Of course she wasn't as clever and
witty as I am, but you couldn't fault her for trying.*

She shook her head. "I haven't seen Ilie since I left your
house. I'll keep an eye out for him though."

"Thanks," Nick said as he handed her the last of the envelopes.

She nodded and started back down the street. She was still a
little wobbly but was basically heading in the right direction.

Nick sighed and glared down into his pocket at me.

"Hey," I yelled. "Don't look at me in that tone of voice!"

"'They're just around the corner,'" he mocked. "Sure thing,
McGee."

I gave kind of a sheepish shrug and confessed, "I guess my
Tracking Globule needs a little, uh . . . re-globulating."

119

With the Tracking Globule now history, Nick expanded his search into the business district. He even swung by Dad's office building and later checked the dumpster, where they had run into Crazy Jim.

No Ilie . . . no Michael . . . For that matter, no Crazy Jim, either.

Nick began stopping people on the street and asking them if they'd seen Michael and Ilie. Again, no response . . . unless you count the old lady who clobbered him with her umbrella 'cause she thought he was a mugger.

By the time evening rolled around, Nick had given up hope. He slowly trudged home. His feet were killing him, but that was nothing compared to the pain in the middle of his chest.

At that exact moment somebody else was trudging home. . . .

It was dark under the freeway bridge as Steven found the hole in the chain link fence and squeezed through. He began running. He had to. His mom had expected him hours ago.

Cars and trucks rumbled overhead as he passed one giant freeway pylon after another. Finally he came upon their old station wagon. Next to it was a collection of refrigerator boxes and pieces of cardboard that made up his family's home.

At least, they *called* it home . . . because that's where they lived. But everyone else would say they were homeless, because a car and a bunch of boxes was no place for anybody to live.

Still, it had been a good day for Steven. He had managed to hit a McDonald's dumpster twice at just the right time. That meant he not only had plenty of half-eaten Breakfast Burritos, but lots of pieces of Quarter Pounders and Chicken McNuggets, too.

"It's Stevie!" his two little sisters called as he poked his head inside the cardboard. "Mom! It's Stevie!"

They jumped up and greeted him. Of course, it wasn't just him they were interested in. It was also the sack he carried and whatever surprises he might have found and stuffed into his pockets for them. Why, just yesterday he'd brought back a rubber dinosaur and a small stuffed penguin.

"Whatcha got? Whatcha got?" they asked, digging into his pockets and reaching for the sack.

"Go away!" he shouted, shaking them off. "I got no toys today, just food."

"Where have you been?" his mother demanded. There was no missing the fear in her voice.

Steven looked up and swallowed. She hovered over him, glowering.

"I've been gettin' . . . stuff," he said, holding out the McDonald's sack to her. "I had to swing by the college snack bar to microwave it to kill all the germs."

She snatched the sack out of his hand. "You're supposed to be home before dark. You know that! There's all sorts of ugly people out there. What if . . ." Suddenly her voice started to crack. "What if . . ." She could no longer continue. She could only reach out and pull him into her arms. So much for anger. Now, it was a time for tears.

"I'm sorry, Mom . . ."

"I-I know it's . . . hard," she stammered, pressing her

cheek against his head. "I know you want to do all you can to help. But you . . . you've got to be more careful . . . you've *got* to!"

She held him for a long moment—almost afraid to let him go. Finally she released him. "Now go wash up," she ordered, straightening herself and wiping her eyes. She turned to her two daughters, pretending nothing had happened. "Girls, help me set the table."

They grumbled and complained as they stepped outside and washed their hands in the plastic paint bucket they refilled each day from a local fire hydrant.

Outside, Steven noticed his dad sitting on a folding lawn chair. He was by a little fire, staring into the flames. It was dangerous having a fire. If some official saw it, he could run the family off again. But they had no choice. It would get down to freezing again tonight, and they needed the heat.

"How'd it go?" Steven asked as he joined his dad and warmed his hands.

The man let out a slow sigh as he wrapped his arm around Steven's waist. "No job . . . not yet."

Steven nodded. His dad had changed a lot over the months. But what hurt Steven the most was his jokes. Or, actually, the lack of them. A year ago his dad had had a joke for everything. True, most of them were groaners, but they'd been fun to listen to. Now . . . well, let's just say Steven missed the jokes the most.

"I didn't do too bad," Steven said trying to sound cheery. "I got some food, and look—" He pulled a compass out of his pocket. "I found this so we won't get lost."

"That's fine, Stevie," his dad said, patting him on the

shoulder. "I can always count on you." He threw a quick glance toward Steven's mom, who had also stepped outside. He pulled his son closer and whispered, "But don't be gone so long anymore . . . for Mom's sake. She was pretty worried."

"I'm sorry," Steven said.

A long moment of silence hung between the two. Finally Steven spoke again. "Dad . . . tomorrow's Thanksgiving, isn't it?"

"Yes," the man answered quietly.

"Are we gonna do anything, you know, special for it?"

His dad stared back into the fire. "Maybe . . . I don't know. At the moment we're a little short on things to be thankful for."

Then, without a word, the man rose and took a few steps away. He was either examining the darkness or trying to keep his son from seeing his tears. It wasn't hard to guess which.

Finally he sighed and turned back to Steven. "I guess we do have a few things to be thankful for. At least we're all together." With that he turned and headed for the table.

Actually, "the table" was just another large box on its side. Steven's mom had set out some old plastic plates. On them were scattered pieces of Steven's take from McDonald's.

"Dad?" Steven asked as they sat down. "I met this strange man today. He had a beard and—"

"I told you never to speak to strangers," his mother interrupted.

"I didn't say a word," Steven insisted. "But he handed

123

this to me." He took off his shoe and pulled out a ten-dollar bill from inside.

Everyone stared in amazement.

"A stranger gave that to you?" his mom asked.

"Yeah," Steven said, nodding. "And then he disappeared into the crowd—almost like he was a ghost or something."

His mom took the money. "A ghost!" she said, grinning. "Pretty rich for a ghost."

"Maybe he was an angel!" the oldest sister cried.

"He was real nice," Steven said. "Didn't say a word 'till the end, and then it was kinda strange."

"What'd he say that was so strange?" his mom asked.

"He said, 'Trust God . . . you're not alone.'"

"Probably one of those religious fanatics bribing you to believe in God," his dad said with a loud snort. "God . . . there is no God! Not for us." He paused for a moment, then said, "But he's right about one thing. We're not alone--we got each other."

Steven glanced up at his dad, then to his mom. Finally he looked to the beams of moving light that spilled down from the freeway over their heads. His dad was right. They weren't alone, they did have each other.

But somehow, Steven suspected that the stranger meant more than that. A lot more. . . .

SEVEN
Spy-Tracker

Back at home, Nick felt pretty low. He put on his pajamas, then sat (more like drooped) at his art table. He stared vacantly at his drawing pad. Maybe if he doodled something . . . put ol' McGee into an adventure, maybe then he could pull himself out of this slump.

He picked up his pencil, but it felt like a lead brick. Not a good sign. Then his eyes fell on the cup Ilie gave him. It was still on the floor where he'd thrown it when Ilie had run away.

Nicholas crossed over and picked it up. Once again he looked at its intricate designs. *All that carving must've taken Ilie a long time,* he thought. Finally Nick noticed an inscription on the bottom:

"To Nick, my best American friend . . . Ilie."

As if that wasn't bad enough, Nicholas spotted something else. Just below the inscription were more letters. Painted. He pronounced the syllables out loud as he put them together. "Car . . . pai . . . thi . . . a."

He repeated the name, almost shouting, *"Carpaithia!"*

Nicholas's stomach dropped to the floor. Ilie had made the pencil cup out of his prized model ship! The one he had talked about when they were examining Nick's red glider.

It was a low blow. The lowest. And Nicholas knew he'd given it to himself.

"Man . . . ," he groaned. "I really messed up."

Suddenly I popped up out of the drawing pad. "Yeah," I said, trying to sound sympathetic. "Now you know how a turkey feels on Thanksgiving."

OK, OK, so I'm not the world's most sympathetic friend, but with my terrific looks, sparkling personality, and perfectly straight teeth . . . let's face it, I'm still as close to perfection as they come, right?

I said, "RIGHT?"

HEY! IS ANYBODY OUT THERE?

I tell ya, for a reader, you're not the most talkative person I've ever met. I guess my greatness can be kinda intimidating sometimes, right?

I said, "RIGHT?"

Oh, forget it.

Nicholas was about to give up, too. "I didn't even give Ilie a chance," he said. "All I could think of was my own, stupid self and that stupid football game." He set the cup down on the table and stared at it. "Now I'll probably never see Ilie again."

"Don't be so sure," I said. "I know a guy who can find anybody."

"Oh, yeah? Who's that?" Nick looked at me suspiciously.

It was now or never. Although I'd known Nicky boy for years, it was time to share my deepest secret. Time to reveal my true identity. Yes, believe it or not, I wasn't just a superiorly gor-

geous hunk of cartoon creativity. That was only a cover, a clever disguise to protect my true identity.

Quicker than you can say, "Oh no! Are we about to do another McGee fantasy?" I whipped out a pair of sunglasses, slid them on, and spoke in my best British accent:

"The name's Blond . . . James Blond."

"Oh, brother," Nick groaned. "McGee, please, I'm not in the mood. . . ."

But he was too late. Already the drawing table was turning into some sleazy street on the sleazy side of the tracks in the sleaziest section of some sleazy European city. You could tell it was in Europe because the police sirens didn't go RRRRRRRRRRrrrrrr . . . ; they went Bleeeh-Blaaaah, Bleeeh-Blaaah, Bleeeh-Blaaah.

With the suave elegance, cool detachment, and wry humor only British superspies can use effectively, I pursued my archnemesis, Dimitri Villinov, through the back sleazy streets.

Suddenly a sleazy guy (I think I've used the word sleazy enough, don't you?) in a sleazy trench coat (OK, OK, I promise. No more.) disappeared around a sleaz—uh, a dark and sinister corner.

Quickly I pulled out my incredible Spy-Tracking Globular Device, and (since this is a fantasy) it worked perfectly.

Beep . . . Beep . . . Beep . . .

I was hot on his trail. Like a shadow. Step for step, turn for turn. Any minute and I'd have this notorious, no-good, not-so-nice guy in custody. Just a few more steps and . . .

WOOOOOOOAAAHHHHHHH!

That is obviously the sound of someone falling through an open manhole. An open manhole that drops into a sewer.

SPLAAAAAAASHHHHH!

No need to describe that sound.

But this was no ordinary sewer. No way. We're talking your big-time, state-of-the-smell Toxic Waste Sewer.

But never one to lose my cool or dirty my dinner jacket, I activated my portable All-Purpose-Gadgetron. Quickly I pressed a button on my wrist and . . .

Zoing! Snap, click, click, click—AOOOOGAA!

It completely surrounded me and unfolded into a one-man submarine. (What I won't think of next, huh?) Being an expert submarine pilot, I carefully steered my craft through the gunk and back up to the surface.

But that is not the end. Oh no, dear reader. Flip ahead, and you'll see we still have several more pages to go.

Once out of the obnoxiously odious ooze, the All-Purpose-Gadgetron changed into . . .

Zoing! Snap, click, click, click—VAROOM, VAROOM!

. . . A jet-powered motorcycle.

I hopped aboard, zoomed out of the alley, and back onto the street. As luck would have it there was Villinov straight ahead. The dastardly criminal was carrying two packages into a nearby building. They were either plastic explosives or Girl Scout Cookies (sometimes it's hard to tell the difference). Fearing the worst, I roared toward the door.

Unfortunately, a big-rig truck was also roaring . . . right at your beloved hero! Would this be it? Would this be my last caper? Would I go the route of Maxwell Smart and all the other great spies—lost forever in Nickelodeon reruns?

Fear not. There was still one last button on my Gadgetron. With the blinding speed of a touch typist, I punched the key. Suddenly . . .

ZOING! Snap, click, click, click—ROOOOAR, WOOOSH!

. . . the cycle turned into a rocket-powered hang glider. Just before I and the eighteen-wheeler become inseparable buddies, I roared high into the air, out of harm's way.

Now, flying above the street, I spied Villinov's silhouette through a fifteenth-story window, along with a bunch of other silhouettes. Obviously there was a secret meeting of totally tasteless and terrible troublemakers in the making. I banked my glider and zoomed in. Seconds later I exploded through the window and sent the leader flying across the room.

"Hope I'm not crashing your party," I said smoothly.

"Thatza exactly what you'vea done!" the man sneered in an Italian accent.

Great Scott! I had created one of history's greatest moments. Yes, believe it or not, the great me had actually made a mistake. It was not Villinov, the Soviet's greatest secret spy. It was Guido, your average, run-of-the-mill pizza delivery guy.

And the other members of his secret meeting were not members of anything. They were all astonished partygoers, holding little wiener thingies on toothpicks and staring at me.

Uh-ohhh . . .

They began to complain, then yell, then wave their toothpicks menacingly at your true-blue hero. Before becoming their next appetizer, I apologized—"So sorry, old chaps"—and prepared to leave.

But not before helping myself to a nearby tray of drinks. "Ahh, Chateau Co-lah '93—shaken, not stirred." I announced as I grabbed a pop can, shook it, and popped it open.

Unfortunately, fizz showered over everyone. Suddenly they

were all soaked. Really soaked. Not only were they soaked, but they were steamed.

"GET HIM!" they screamed.

The entire crowd began chasing me around the banquet table. Guido thought he'd join in the fun, too, by throwing one pizza after another at me.

Suddenly I heard laughing. Well, not really laughing, but smiling. OK, so I didn't hear smiling, I saw it. The point is my little fantasy was dissolving. Before I knew it I was standing back on the art table. I glanced over to Nick. His mood had definitely lightened. . . .

"Thanks for the thought," he said, chuckling as he reached for the light. "But I think this is one mystery I'll have to solve on my own."

The light went out.

But not before a pizza the size of the national debt flew in from the sketch pad and nailed me in the kisser.

"Hooo-hooo-hooo," somebody laughed in an Italian accent. (I just hate smart-aleck fantasies that don't know when to end, don't you?)

"McGee?" Nick asked from his bed. "Did you say something?"

"Naw," I grumbled as I pulled the stringy pizza from my face. "I'm just having a little bedtime snack."

The next morning Thanksgiving blew in, cold and windy. At least it wasn't snowing. Of course, that disappointed all the kids with sleds and cozy fireplaces. But for Steven and his family it was a relief. Cardboard doesn't hold up well under snow.

Unfortunately, the weather was about the only good thing that morning. Holidays meant empty fast-food dumpsters . . . which meant empty stomachs. Steven had been out on the streets all morning and had found nothing.

Still, he couldn't shake the feeling that something good was going to happen. He remembered the man who had given him the ten dollars. He could still picture the look of kindness in his eyes. He could still hear the voice: "Trust God . . . you're not alone."

What did he mean? Was he an angel? Who was he talking about? God?

Eventually Steven found himself in front of a restaurant. It was torture. Besides the incredible smells, the windows were painted with pictures to advertise their Thanksgiving Dinner Special. Pictures of turkey and dressing, sweet potatoes, and pies piled high with whipped cream.

Steven leaned his forehead against the window and peered in. Inside there were dining tables, a long soup and salad bar, and double doors that swung open and shut as serving people brought out trays of food. Any minute the restaurant would be open for business. Any minute he might be able to—

Suddenly a large face appeared in the window before him. Steven jumped in fright.

"Get away from here!" the muffled voice cried from behind the glass. "Get away, or I'm calling the cops!"

Steven turned and walked quickly down the street. His eyes started to smart with tears. His anger burned. "I'm no thief," he muttered. "Can't a guy even look?" Again he thought of the man with the ten dollars. Again he remembered what he had said. *You are not alone.*

131

Ha! Who was the man kidding? Steven *was* alone. All alone! There was no angel. There was no God. There was just him. Alone.

Then he heard something. At first he couldn't make it out. He wiped his eyes and followed the sound into a nearby alley.

Somebody was singing—lots of somebodies.

It grew louder and louder. Finally, he spotted the door with a cross above it. Several people stood in front singing and warmly greeting other people.

It's a mission, Steven thought. He'd heard about them. His mom and dad had told him to stay away from them. His shoulders sagged as he turned back . . . until a friendly voice from behind cried, "Hello!"

Steven whirled around to see a boy his size standing with a grocery sack full of bread loaves. "Vould you like to come eenside?" the boy asked brightly.

As you may have guessed, this was no ordinary boy. This was Ilie. In spite of Nick's harsh words, Ilie still hadn't lost his sparkle.

Steven looked at him a moment, then he shook his head. "No, thanks," he said. "My mom told me not to go into . . . places like that."

"Why?" Ilie looked puzzled. "It costs you nothing and—"

"Look, I don't know," Steven said, backing away. "It's just that . . . well, we won't join your . . . uh . . . group just for a handout."

"Oh!" Ilie nodded. "I see. Zat's what your parents told you, eh?"

"Yeah . . . uh . . . now I have to get home and . . ." He turned to leave.

"But eets not like that at all," Ilie called to him. "We just want to help. Jesus healed and fed and helped people, and he told us to do ze same. He cares, so we care, too."

Steven turned back to Ilie. Was this guy for real? Where were the strings? What did he *really* want?

Ilie continued, "And, since we believe Jesus ees greatest gift of all, you can't blame us for we want to share him with you. After all," he said, "you are not alone."

Steven froze. There was that phrase again. The same one the man who gave him the money had used. Not only that, but as Steven looked into Ilie's eyes, he saw the same expression he had seen on the man's face: a look of kindness mixed with joy and love. It was eerie, but Steven knew it was no accident. He hesitated, unsure.

"Come inside. I show you," Ilie said, gesturing toward the mission. Then he leaned in and whispered, "Besides, ze food ees terrific. I help cook it myself." He winked and Steven smiled.

The two of them started toward the door, then Steven suddenly stopped. "What about my family?" he asked. "I should go get them."

"Come eenside, first," Ilie said, "then you will have more to tell them when you go get them."

Again Steven smiled. He couldn't help it. Something about Ilie's joy was contagious.

They went up to the door, past the singers, past Michael, who was grinning and playing his mandolin . . . and they finally stepped inside.

133

EIGHT
A Day for Turkeys

Over in Nicholas's neighborhood it was pretty much Thanksgiving as usual. Leaves fluttered from the sky like red and yellow confetti. The backyard Nick had raked so carefully a couple of days earlier was already covered in a thick new carpet.

And inside . . . inside it was your typical pre–Thanksgiving dinner craziness. The TV blared with parades (and cartoon-character balloons the size of Kansas). And then there was football. Lots of football. Lots and lots of football.

But not for the womenfolk. No sir. To the women, football was peanuts! Mom, Sarah, and Grandma had their own Olympic-type of athletics going as they ran around the kitchen madly preparing the dinner.

"I can't believe Michael and Ilie took off like that," Mom muttered as she poked her head in the oven to check on the bread.

About this time Jamie's intercom buzzed.

Mom jerked up to answer but forgot to pull her head out of the oven first.

BAM!

(If you thought that sounded like a mother's head hitting the top of an oven, you're right.)

"Mom," Jamie's voice whined through the intercom. "How soon is dinner? I'm hungry! Can you bring me something to eat?"

"I'll see what I can do," Mom answered, rubbing her head. She glanced at all the food on the counter. "We have enough to feed the entire Marine Corps. I'm sure we can find you something."

Grandma crossed from the table, looking a little harried. "What shall I do with the Romanian cabbage casserole?"

"Put it on the table," Mom said, heading for the pantry. "After all that work, we're at least going to try it." She snatched some crackers and cheese spread and started for Jamie's room.

Meanwhile, Nicholas was up in his room feeling about as worthless as used dental floss. On a scale of one to ten, his self-esteem was about .0000000000001.

When Mom walked in, he was lying on his bed, staring up at his glider.

"Nick, come on downstairs," she said with a sigh. "We're almost ready."

But Nicholas didn't move. "I'm not hungry," he murmured with the enthusiasm of a drugged zombie.

"Not hungry?" she playfully scorned as she crossed over to him. "I fixed enough food for an army! And with Ilie and Michael gone, I'm counting on *you* to at least eat the cabbage casserole!" She poked her finger at his ribs.

But Nick didn't smile. He barely moved. He just lay there, his eyes focused on intergalactic nothingness. "I really messed up, didn't I?" he mumbled. "He was my friend and I treated him like . . ."

"We all did," Mom said as she took a deep breath. "Sometimes life starts moving so fast that we forget to love others. We think only of ourselves."

"I'm really sorry . . ."

Again Mom sighed. "So am I, honey, so am I."

A half hour later the family was gathered around the dining table. With all the extra extension leaves put into it, the table was about the size of an aircraft carrier. (And with all the food piled on top of it, it also weighed about as much as a carrier.)

Everyone wore their best duds. When they sat down, though, two seats were still empty—Jamie's (thanks to the measles) and Dad's (thanks to the football game still on the tube).

"David!" Mom called.

But Dad didn't hear. His team was down by a field goal, and there was only one minute to go. Perched on the edge of his seat, his eyes wide, his adrenaline pumping, Dad watched as the announcer shouted, "He's at the forty! . . . the thirty! . . . the—"

Suddenly the screen went blank.

"What? Hey!" Dad exploded . . . until he saw Mom holding the remote. One look at her face told him this was not the time to protest. The meal had been three days in the making and would take another three days to clean up. It was going to be eaten when it was hot *or Mom's name wasn't Mom!*

Dad swallowed nervously. "Not waiting on me, I

hope?" he asked sheepishly as he crossed to the table and took his seat.

After everyone got settled, Dad turned to his son and asked, "Nicholas, will you give thanks for us?"

"Me?" Nick looked up in surprise. The last thing he wanted to do was pray. After what he'd pulled, who was he to pray for anything or anybody?

Dad nodded for him to go ahead.

The family took one another's hands, and, reluctantly, Nick bowed his head. It took a moment for the words to come. "I'm thankful," he croaked, "that I, uh . . . had a friend like Ilie. And maybe, with your help, he'll be able to . . . forgive me for what I did."

Nick paused a moment as if searching his thoughts.

Sarah coughed slightly to remind him she'd like to eat before Christmas.

Finally, he continued. "Bless him . . . and bless this food. Amen."

For a moment Nick didn't look up. Then he felt the squeeze of understanding coming from Mom's hand. He looked over to her, and she smiled. He tried to return it.

"All right," Grandma said as she reached for the mashed potatoes and started to pass them. "Let's get this meal on the road."

Suddenly there was a loud knock at the window.

Everyone jumped and turned toward it. The last time this had happened it had been in the middle of the night, and the mystery knockers had been Michael and Ilie. This time it was the middle of the day and it was . . . Michael and Ilie!

Nicholas leaped from his seat and raced toward the door.

"Theyyyy're baaaacckkk!" Sarah announced ominously.

Nick flung open the back door. He couldn't believe it. There they were, just like on the first night. God was giving him another chance!

"No answer to bell," Michael said with a shrug, "so we come to back." They stepped gingerly inside as though nothing had gone wrong—as though the last twenty-four hours had never happened.

"I thought . . . I . . . ," Nick stammered, confused. "Where were you guys?!"

Michael and Ilie exchanged puzzled looks as the rest of the family rose to join them.

"Didn't you get note?" Michael asked, rummaging through his pockets. "I am sure I left note for you—" he pulled a crumpled piece of paper from his pocket—"een my own pocket?" he finished weakly.

Everyone chuckled.

"My friends, please forgive me," he said with an embarrassed look. "Yesterday, Ilie and I, we go to Back Alley Mission to help feed peoples who have not enough food and—"

"You've been doing volunteer work all this time?" Dad interrupted.

Ilie nodded in excitement.

"Please," Dad said, gesturing to the table, "grab a chair and join us."

Michael obeyed wholeheartedly. "So many peoples to feed," he said with a sigh, "and so few to help feed them.

We like to do what we could, to share what we have, just like Meesus Martin said."

"Like I said?" Mom asked in surprise.

"Yes, Meesus Martin," Ilie agreed. For some reason he was still at the window looking outside. "Before, een kitchen, when I hear you tell Julia, ze mail carrier, how Thanksgiving ees a time of sharing good fortune with others, I think then you are very wise."

"So, een suitcase," Michael continued, "we bring clothes to share with those who have not enough to wear."

"You gave away your clothes?" Nick asked in amazement. He didn't know what it was like in Romania, but around here you were what you wore. To give up your clothes was like giving up a piece of yourself.

"Ah, but we also receive!" Michael exclaimed, holding up Crazy Jim's tattered hat. "Just like Indiana Jones, no?"

"More like Indiana James," Nick said, taking the rumpled hat from him and looking it over.

Suddenly Ilie had spotted what he was looking for. "Papa, they are coming!"

"Who are coming?!" Mom asked, glancing from one to the other. There was no missing the hint of concern crossing her face.

Ilie opened the door and called out, "Back here everybody!"

"I will explain," Michael said, walking over to Mom. "As you say, we eenvite people we meet—neighbors, friends . . ."

"You invited . . . people?" Mom asked, her concern turning to dismay.

140

"No worries," Michael reassured her. "Knowing of Meesus Martin's spirit of giving, I say to pastor at mission, 'I know where to send extra peoples when mission run out of room.'"

"Oh, Michael," Mom said with a panicked look, "I wish I'd known sooner. . . ."

"Did someone mention food?" a voice called from the doorway. Everyone looked. Crazy Jim sauntered inside. In his hands was a foil-covered turkey the size of the Goodyear blimp. Behind him were a couple of mission workers carrying boxes of paper plates, utensils, and roasting pans full of even more food.

Mom smiled in relief, then moved into action. She quickly cleared the counter and the table to make a buffet area.

Meanwhile, Grandma and Sarah went to work laying out the plates and utensils.

Nick poked his head out the door and saw a line of poor and homeless types following the food carriers.

"Hey, guys!" he shouted to his family. "We've got company . . . and how!"

"Come right on in," Mom said, greeting the folks at the door. Many of them wore torn and dirty clothing. Some smelled like they hadn't taken a shower in a week. Others looked like it had been that long since they'd had a decent meal. But none of this stopped Mom. In fact, it gave her all the more reasons to smile and direct the people toward the makeshift buffet on the counter.

While she did so, Nick and Dad busily collected chairs, stools, even upside-down buckets—anything for their guests to sit on. Just then, a familiar face pushed through the crowd toward Grandma. "Mrs. Martin?" It was Julia, the mail carrier, and with her was her roommate!

Meanwhile, Dad had turned and found himself face-to-face with Crazy Jim—the man he had given a quarter to just the day before.

"Splendid party, old boy," Crazy Jim said. He reached into his pocket and handed Dad a quarter. "Here's a little something to help with the expenses." He grinned. "I presume you can break a quarter?"

Suddenly Dad remembered why the man looked so familiar, and his face turned beet red as he recalled his stinginess the day before. With a chuckle, Crazy Jim flipped the quarter into the air. Dad caught it, and to help lighten the moment, he managed to find a dime to give back. Now both men laughed.

It would be a long time before Dad forgot the little lesson he learned that day.

Come to think of it, it would be a long time before anyone in the family forgot what they learned.

NINE
Wrapping Up

A few minutes later Nick returned from his room upstairs. In his hand was the model glider that had been hanging above his bed.

"Ilie," he shouted as he threaded his way through the crowd of people. "I want you to have this."

The Romanian boy's eyes widened. "Oh, Nick," he said, backing away, "I cannot accept thees."

"Please," Nick insisted, pushing the glider into Ilie's hands, "I want you to have it. It's just my way of . . . what I mean is, I'm sorry for . . ."

"Eet ees OK, Nick," Ilie said, smiling. "If you had come to visit me during World Cup, I would have thought you were 'Dweeb-O-Matic,' too."

Nick broke into a grin and gave the smaller boy a quick hug.

Michael looked across the room and saw the two boys hugging. "Ahh, Meesus Martin," he chortled, "I see your son has learned well our way of greeting, yes?"

"We've all learned a lot from you," Mom said as she set a stack of dishes in the sink. "I want to thank you for reminding us what Thanksgiving is really about."

"You're welcome!" Michael said with his big laugh.

"Een Romania, I think we should start such a holiday . . . 'Day to be thankful!' Every day we should be thankful, no?"

Mom nodded.

He went on jokingly, "I do not know where we will get the Indians and the Pilgrims, though, but this," he said, pointing to the cabbage casserole, "ees a good start. A greater American dish I never have had!"

After a moment of stunned silence, Mom broke into delighted laughter.

Several hours later, Jamie carefully made her way down the stairs. Who knows how many times she'd buzzed her intercom before finally giving up. At last she appeared on the kitchen stairway wearing her robe, sunglasses (measles don't like bright lights), and gobs of white goop to help stop the itching.

By now most of the guests were gone. But not the pans and plates piled high in the sink.

"Man," she muttered, "I get sick for a few days and look what happens! My family opens a restaurant." She tilted down her sunglasses for a better look. "I better get well . . . fast!"

Suddenly Steven appeared. It's hard to guess who was the more surprised: Jamie, seeing a strange kid in worn-out clothing standing in the middle of her kitchen, or Steven, seeing the white-gooped monster-face dressed in sunglasses and a robe.

Jamie was the first to speak. "Who are you?" she demanded. Then she scowled. "You look awful."

"So what's *your* excuse?" Steven shot back. "Premature acne?"

He stepped up for a closer look.

"Stay back!" she ordered. "Can't you tell, I've got the measles! She took off her sunglasses and explained, "These are for protecting my eyes, and this stuff—" she pointed to the goop on her face—"is to keep the bumps from itching so much."

"Measles." Steven shrugged. "I already had them . . . last spring. No problem. The chicken pox, though, that was bad news! I was one gigantic bag of itch."

Not to be outdone it was Jamie's turn to brag. "Chicken pox?! Kid's stuff. I had strep throat last winter, and you wouldn't believe the—"

She was interrupted by a couple of tattered street people heading toward the back door.

"What's going on?" she demanded. "Am I in an old 'Twilight Zone' rerun?"

"Your mom and dad invited us, you know, from the Back Alley Mission."

"You mean you're . . . homeless people?" Jamie asked, looking at him like he was from Jupiter.

"Don't call me that!" he said threateningly. "I got a family, and we got a home!" He paused for a minute, a little ashamed of his outburst. He shrugged and continued, "Though it ain't much of a home." Then he brightened. "But it won't be that way for long."

"How come?" Jamie asked.

"Because your dad and mom promised to help my dad find work." He suddenly broke out laughing. "Your mom was so funny!"

145

"Mom? Funny?" Jamie asked skeptically. Moms are for feeding you, making you clean up your room, and checking over your homework—not for being funny.

"Yeah!" Steven grinned. "She turned all red when she found out we were living in refrigerator boxes. I thought she was gonna slug somebody. Then she grabbed my mom and yanked her outta the room, jabbering about some nice old Indian down the street—a Mr. Ravenhill who has a whole house to himself."

"Steven!" a voice suddenly called from the back door.

Jamie turned to look as a woman entered. She must have been Steven's mom, 'cause it looked like they shopped at the same store: "Threads 'R' Us."

"It's all set, sweetheart," his mother said. "Mr. Ravenhill is more than willing for us to stay with him. We'd better get going, though, before it gets dark."

"Great!" Steven called. Then turning back to Jamie he shrugged. "Guess we'll see you around."

"Yeah . . . sure."

Jamie watched as the kid headed out the door to join his family. He seemed a nice enough guy. And if he was going to stay at Mr. Ravenhill's place for a while, they'd be like neighbors. Maybe they'd even become friends. Who knew.

Jamie sighed, gave a little scratch around her collar and headed back up the steps.

As Jamie girl headed up the stairs, I figured it was time for me to do a little "heading up" of my own. But not by mere mortal foot power, no-siree-bob. Instead, it would be my magnificent McGee Mind Power. . . .

146

I stood on the middle of the dining-room table and blew into a giant hose attached to an even gianter blimp. Not that I'm full of hot air, mind you, but with this spy business on the downturn, I was looking into new career opportunities. Anything to allow me to use all my fancy-schmanzy surveillance cameras and stuff.

And what could be smarter than making a fortune with my special "McGee-Cam."

I finished inflating the blimp, pulled out the hose, and shoved a giant cork into the hole.

Now I was ready.

Step aside Goodyear—it was time for the new and improved . . . McGee-Year blimp. I would be the one videotaping all the bowl games; I would be the one covering all the parades; I would be the one squeezing his magnificently pudgy body into that magnificently small passenger cabin . . .

Aaagh, Ugggh, Romf . . . Ahhhh . . .

Home, sweet matchbox. I don't want to say the passenger compartment was small, but it was the first time I could scratch my foot by blinking my eyelids.

I pulled anchor, and the blimp began to rise. Faster and faster. Higher and higher. Soon we were millions of miles above the dining-room table.

OK, make that thousands of feet.

All right, all right. But eighteen inches is better than nothing.

The point is, I could see everything . . . well, at least the important things, like every ounce of leftover food. Carefully, I maneuvered the blimp's controls. Talk about complicated. It was worse than Dad's new TV remote. I had no idea what I *was doing. But since when has that ever stopped me, the great McGee?*

And then I saw it. Ah yes, the remains of our turkey. Actually, it was a bird's-eye view of the turkey. (Get it? Turkey? Bird's-eye? I suppose you think you could do better?)

Unfortunately, I was so impressed by my incredible wit (it takes so little to impress me!) that I didn't notice the way the little cork in the blimp had started to work its way out of the not-so-little hole.

Quicker than you can ask, "How many times have I seen this in Saturday morning cartoons?" the cork popped out, and I began zipping around the room.

"Yeeoooooooow!" I cried, hanging on for dear life.

Any fool knew I had to pull up on the controls to keep the blimp's nose pointed toward the sky. So I did what any fool would do. I grabbed the controls and pushed them straight down. (Some people can't tell their lefts from their rights. Well, I can't tell my ups from my downs.) Soon I had that blimp in the world's steepest nosedive.

"Mayday! Mayday!" I cried. "I'm goin' in! I'm goin' in!"
I couldn't have been more right. . . .
SPLAT!
I did "go in." Right into the bowl of gravy.
A moment later I surfaced, covered in the thick brown goo. But every cloud has a silver lining. This stuff was . . .
SLURP . . .
. . . pretty tasty.
GLUG, GLUG, GLUG . . .
With any luck I'd have it all drunk by . . .
CHUG, CHUG, CHUG . . .
. . . my next exciting little adventure.

148

Stay tuned, food fanatics. Who knows what tasty treat of an adventure lies ahead? Who knows what this king of the junk food junkies will eat next? Freeze-dried asparagus with chocolate sauce? Dill pickles covered in Dijon mustard? The mind staggers with possibilities. The stomach retches with nausea.

But first things first. Now it's just me and this bowl of gravy. Hey, it's like I always say, "Into every bowl of gravy, a little turkey must fall."

Ho-ho, ha-ha, hee-hee . . .

BURP!!

See ya around!

Men judge by outward appearance, but [God looks] at a man's thoughts and intentions. (1 Samuel 16:7, *The Living Bible*)

The Blunder Years

by Bill Myers and Robert E. West

ONE
Beginnings

It was worse than twenty-four hours of nonstop Brady Bunch
*reruns. More terrifying than cleaning out the bottom of your
gym locker. More disgusting than lima beans in cream gravy.*

Well, maybe not that bad, but close.

*Nicky boy was trying something new as he sketched in my
beautiful baby blues and fantastically fabulous face. I wanted
to move around and see what he was up to, but since he hadn't
drawn my legs yet, moving anywhere was a little on the impos-
sible side.*

"Whatcha up to, buddy boy?" I shouted.

*No answer. He just kept sketching. At last he got around to
my magnificent bod—that renowned hunk of handsomeness
that causes women around the world to swoon in ecstasy, to
scream in hysteria, to beg me never to take off my shirt. . . .*

*I craned my neck for a better look. Nicky's pencil was moving
faster than a little kid making the rounds on Halloween. But
. . . hey! Oh no! Hold the phone . . . could it be? I couldn't
believe my eyes! Nick was trading in my perfect pudginess for
something leaner, meaner, and less huggable.*

He was changing me!

"What are you doin'?" I shouted. "That ain't me!"

153

Instead of giving me an answer, he quickly sketched in a button-down collar.

"What?"

Then a pinkie ring the size of a Buick.

"Nick??"

Suddenly I was wearing pleated pants.

"NICHOLAS!!"

And saddle shoes.

"AUGH!"

Then . . . horror of horrors, worst of worsts, catastrophe of catastrophes! No, we aren't talkin' world hunger or thermonuclear war. We aren't even talkin' collapse of the universe. It was worse. Much worse.

We're talkin' about changing my hair!!!

"No, Nicholas! Not the—"

I was too late. Suddenly my golden locks were replaced with an Elvis Presley hairdo. Then, before I could croon out a quick "You ain't nothin' but a hound dog," Nick's pencils started scratching and filling the rest of me in with loud, obnoxious colors.

"Cut it out, kid, that tickles!"

He didn't cut it out. He just kept going until he was done. I looked down at his work. . . . AUUGGHHH!

"What's going on?" I screamed. "I look like a game show host!"

"Lighten up, McGee," Nick scolded. "We're in junior high now. We gotta get a new look. Make a statement. Be hip."

"Hip-schmip!" I cried as I tried to slip out of my clothes and adjust my oversized, hairspray-stiff hair. "Change me back!"

"OK." Nick shrugged as he picked up his eraser. In a minute he'd fixed my hair and had me back into my red, white,

and blues . . . complete with standard issue suspenders and sneakers.

With a sigh of relief, I hopped off the pad and demanded, "What's gotten into you, anyway?"

"Whaddya talking about?" Nick asked. But he wasn't looking at me—he was too busy looking in the mirror and giving his hair a quick work over.

I frowned. Something was up. I strolled over to the edge of the drawing table. "Ever since you started hanging around with that Rex guy at school, you've been acting different!" I insisted.

Nick gave his comb a flick. "That's because Rex Rogers, who happens to be the coolest guy at Eastfield Junior High, is gonna show me what's cool." He dropped his comb into his pocket like a gunfighter holstering his pistol. "In fact, he's coming over in a few."

"A few what?" I asked.

"A few, you know, minutes."

The kid was in worse shape than I thought. If he kept this up, his ego was gonna be bigger than mine. And this house wasn't big enough for that—come to think of it, neither was the universe. I glanced down at my feet. "Augghh! You drew my shoes on backwards." The boy blunder didn't even notice, so I sat down and tried to change them myself. "If you ask me—" I gave my right shoe a tug—"Ughhh! Old Rexy's a little too—uuuuumph!—cool for his own—grrrrr!—good." I finally yanked my shoe off. The only problem was when it went flying, so did I.

"AIEEEEEEEEEEEEEEEE!"

Right into the wastebasket.

I tried to stay cool—though it's a little hard to be cool when *you're standing inside a wastepaper basket covered in pencil shavings, with a Gooey-Chewy Bar wrapper stuck to your rear.*

Nick peered over the edge and did his best not to laugh. "All I know," he said, "is if you wanna be someone in junior high, you gotta be like Rex Rogers."

Right on cue, the door flew open. Nick spun around, accidentally kicking over my trash can and sending me rolling.

"Whoaa!"

Rumble, rumble . . .

"NICHOLAS!"

Rattle, rattle . . .

"N I C H O L A S !!"

. . . roll, roll, roll . . .

He didn't hear my yelling. As I staggered out of the wastebasket, I could see the reason why: Rex Rogers had entered the room. *The* Rex Rogers—the coolest guy this side of a Bugle Boy commercial.

There he stood . . . black jeans, black jacket (complete with pushed-up sleeves), all wrapped around a plain white shirt and socks. And let's not forget those Ray•Bans. Day or night Rexy boy couldn't be seen without his shades. Rumor had it he even wore them in the shower.

"Hey, dude, how's it blow-dryin'?" Rex quipped to his awestruck apprentice.

"Hey, Rexster." Nick fumbled for the words. "Uh . . . stylin' . . . big-time."

I thought I was going to get sick. Since when did Nick start speaking "cool-ese"?

"Cool," Rex answered as he turned to check out the room.

"Cool." Nick nodded.

156

(I tell you, if things got any cooler here we'd start storing sides of beef.)

Rex eyed the world-famous inventions that Nick had hanging around his room. Now it's true, a few of those inventions still needed a little work—like his jet-powered roller skates (which he couldn't slow down to under two hundred miles per hour). Then, of course, there was his solar-powered umbrella (which could only be used on sunny days). And let's not forget his remote-controlled salad spinner. (Hey, it almost worked—'til it confused Dad's green tie for a cucumber.)

I waited for Rex's words of admiration, but instead of praising Nick on all this keen stuff, Mr. Cool just rolled his eyes and gave Nick's remote-controlled dinosaur a kick. "What's with all the kid junk?" Rexy boy complained. "Place looks like Mister Rogers' Neighborhood."

Rex turned toward my drawing table, and Nicholas quickly tossed some of his stuff under his bed. Rexy baby started admiring some of Nick's sketches of me. Well, at least the guy had taste. . . .

Until he opened his mouth.

"Doodles?" he asked, turning back to Nick. "Drawing doodles is very uncool."

DOODLES?! Why, if I was another five feet taller and 180 pounds heavier, I'd show this bozo a thing or two!

Suddenly Rexy spied Nick's open Bible. Nicholas squirmed nervously as Mr. Too Cool crossed over and picked it up to read: "'Men judge by the outward appearance. . . .'" He looked up.

Nick waited for the verdict.

"Cool," Rex finally said. "Very, very cool."

Nicholas heaved a sigh of relief as Rex plopped the book back on the desk and continued his tour of the room.

Hold the phone! How could the Bible say anything this Popsicle could agree with?! I crawled up the chair and onto the desk to take a read for myself. I scanned down the page until I spotted it. Let's see . . . here it is: "Men judge by the outward appearance, but—"

Ahhh-haaa! A "BUT." I knew it!

I continued reading: "But God looks at a man's thoughts and intentions."

Just as I thought. That slicked-down, shady-eyed rooster missed the whole point! I looked up, ready to point this out to Nick, but he wasn't even looking my way. His eyes were glued to Rex, who was continuing his search-and-scorn mission around the room. He'd just discovered one of Nick's model planes and was holding it up like a dirty diaper, giving Nick his famous "meltdown" look.

Nick grabbed a box. "Oh . . . ahh . . . I was just . . . just packing up all this old stuff," he stammered as he threw everything he could grab into the box. "For the . . . the dump, you know."

Suddenly, Jamie, Nick's nine-year-old sister, burst through the door. (Jamie was great at bursting.) "Your Junior Rangers magazine came in the mail," she said, holding it out to him. "I hope you don't mind—I already cut out the recipe for raccoon cookies."

In a flash Nick snatched the magazine from her hand and stuffed it into the "junk" box. Then, before she could complain, he spun her around. "I hate to see you rush out," he said, hustling her toward the door, "but I think it's time for your four o'clock feeding."

"What? But—," she protested. With a slam, she was gone, except for some muffled complaints on the other side of the door. (She was also great at complaining.)

"Little sisters," Nick said with a shrug. "Major drag."

"Yeah." Rex nodded. "Totally juvenile."

There was an awkward moment as Nick tried to think of something else cool to say about his sister. Unfortunately, his folks had brought him up too well to say anything really mean.

"Well, uh . . . I guess we oughta study for that U.S. history test," he finally suggested.

"Bag the books, dude," Rex replied. "What's to study about U.S. history? Christopher Columbus checked the place out. Now we're here."

"Oh yeah . . . right. Well . . . I guess we could . . ." Nick was stumped. I mean, what do cool guys do? Then he had it!

"We could comb our hair!"

"Excellent!" Rex exclaimed. "Yer catchin' on, dude!"

They pulled out their combs and strutted to the mirror.

"Nick! Rex! Dinner!" It was Mom.

Too bad. They were just getting into the real spirit of cool-ness. With heavy sighs they holstered their combs and headed for the door. Rexy-Poo hesitated for one last look in the mirror, but he saw nothing to fix. (If he'd asked me, I could have given him a twenty-page list . . . single spaced . . . with lots of footnotes.)

He swiveled around and joined Nick. They headed out the door without so much as a "Catch ya later, dude" to yours truly.

I hopped into my sketch pad and strolled over to my kitchen. Needless to say, I was pretty upset about everything and figured it was time to have a good think. And what's a good think *without half a dozen bags of Chee•tos, twelve Hostess Ho-Hos, and four diet Cokes? (I like to nibble when I noodle.) The best I figured, ol' Nicky boy was in for another lesson of life.*

Too bad. I just hoped it wouldn't be too painful. And, of course, that he'd leave my hair alone. . . .

TWO
Losers, Weepers

While Nick and Rex were making swirlies in their hair, Mom and Jamie were downstairs putting supper on the table. Actually, Mom was "putting," Jamie was "tossing."

When Mom told her little girl to set the table, she didn't mean for Jamie to deal out the plates. But the nine-year-old had those plates skidding across the table into place faster than Las Vegas's best dealers. Just then, Sarah flung open the door and charged into the room with her tennis racket.

"Sarah!" Jamie cried, as she ran around the table to her. "Did you ask the other players?"

"Jamie," Sarah sighed, as she flung her racket onto the couch. "You cannot be our tennis team mascot." Jamie gave a frustrated huff and returned to the table, where she started dealing out the knives and forks.

Sarah slumped into a nearby chair. "Anyway, why would you wanna be a mascot for a team that has exactly zero wins this century?" She propped her chin dejectedly on her elbow.

"Lost again?" Mom asked sympathetically.

"I'll say. I don't know why they use the word *love* when

you don't score any points. It's more like total humiliation."

It was about this time that Nick and Rex ambled into the room. "Hey, Mom," Nick drawled in his coolest of cool voices. "We're ready to do dinner."

Mom hesitated a moment. "Good, 'cause I'm almost finished 'doing' salad."

Nick and Rex traded "Get real!" looks. What was an uncool grown-up doing trying to sound like a cool kid? They shrugged and sauntered over to the table. It took one millionth of a second for Rex to focus on Nick's gorgeous big sister.

"So, Sarah," he said as they all took their seats, "it's gonna be, like, only eighteen months before I hit the freshman class. Maybe you and me could get together sometime and make some memories."

Sarah looked at him like he had just dropped in from Pluto. "Sure, Rex," she quipped, wearing her best painted-on smile. "Should I pick you up at your house? Or would you rather have your mommy drop you off here?"

It was one of her better put-downs, but since "super-cool" doesn't necessarily mean "superintelligent," Rex popped up his thumb and grinned. "Excellent!" he said.

"OK," Mom broke in, trying her best to save Rex any more humiliation. "Here we go!" She set a platter full of barbecued chicken and a basket of biscuits in front of them.

"Barbecued Yard Bird?!" Rex announced enthusiastically. "I'm stoked!"

"Huh?" Mom and Jamie asked simultaneously.

162

Nick interpreted with a shrug. "He's excited about the chicken."

Suddenly Dad entered through the kitchen door, briefcase in hand. "Hi, everybody!"

A chorus of hellos greeted him. Even Sarah picked up her chin long enough for a halfhearted "Hi." Mom, of course, gave him a welcome-home kiss as he crossed to take his place at the table.

"Sorry I'm late," he said as he joined them. "I got a late call at the paper, but it was worth it." Wearing a mysterious grin, he paused to tuck in his napkin. Then, looking over the food, he continued, "Ahh . . . nothing like a great meal to celebrate a little great news." He paused again, waiting for a reaction.

"Great news?" Mom asked.

Dad just grinned. He had the "pregnant pause" perfected to a fine art. He'd learned to say just enough to get your ears pricked, then hold off while you sat there, curiosity building second by second until you felt like a boiler about to explode.

"Great news?" Sarah repeated hopefully. She could use a little great news. "What is it, Dad?"

"Patience." He grinned. "First, let's give thanks."

Normally, the Martins are pretty good at praying. They have no problem remembering to thank God for all his love and goodness to them. But when you're busy thinking about "great news" it can be a little hard getting your head bowed and your mind on praying.

For Nick, the problem was doubly bad. After all, here he was with the coolest guy in school at his table, and suddenly he's supposed to bow his head and hold hands?

He wasn't sure about praying, but he knew hand holding with family members was definitely *not* in the "Handbook of Coolness."

Rex didn't have a clue what was going on until little Jamie grabbed his hand. He hesitated, but she was pretty persistent. Then, noticing everyone had bowed their heads, he lowered his.

Dad cleared his voice and began. "For this meal and those who prepared it, we thank you, Lord. Bless our home, and our friend Rex. Amen."

Quick as a flash, Nick dropped the hands he held and flashed a nervous shrug to Rex.

"So, David . . . ," Mom pressed.

"Yes?" Dad asked as he buttered his biscuit.

"The news?" Mom persisted.

"What news is that?" Dad teased.

"David!"

"Dad!"

He chuckled lightly, then continued. "Well . . . Nick's principal, Mrs. Pryce, called . . . about next week's Twenty-Fifth Annual Battle of the Bands."

"You mean Endless Summer?" Nick interrupted excitedly, forgetting that cool guys don't get excited. "It's supposed to be the most awesome Battle the school's ever had." Suddenly a disturbing thought crossed his mind. "Tell me you're not chaperons!"

"Even better!" Dad grinned. "You see, twenty-five years ago, when your mom and I were eighth graders at Eastfield, the first Battle of the Bands was . . . well . . . our idea."

"Prehistoric, dude," Rex whispered to Nick.

"Well," Dad went on, "the good news is that they've asked us to come back and host this year's Battle."

Mom came unglued. She shrieked with delight and practically knocked Dad off his chair with her hug.

The other reactions in the room were somewhat mixed.

Sarah congratulated them (grateful that they were hosting an event for the junior high and not the senior high). Jamie was confused just trying to come to grips with the idea that Mom and Dad had ever been in the eighth grade.

And Nick? Well, he looked like he had just swallowed last year's cafeteria special—"hashloaf surprise"—definitely green around the gills. "You're ho . . . ho . . . hosting?" he choked.

"That's right." Dad beamed. "This year's Battle of the Bands is going to be a Martin family affair!"

"Oh, Nick," Mom giggled, "aren't you just . . . just . . ." She tried desperately to think of a word her son could relate to. A word that would help him share her excitement: "Aren't you just stoked?!"

Nick stared at her, his face green, his mouth ajar. Well, so much for sharing.

Rex leaned over to him and murmured, "This is starting to sound more like endless bummer."

"Endless bummer" was exactly what Sarah's life on the tennis court had become.

Three days later she was again dancing from foot to foot, waiting for the final, match-point serve. It came.

She returned it beautifully.

The opposition fired it back across at Tina, Sarah's best friend and doubles partner. She fended it off perfectly.

So far, so good.

The fuzzy little ball kept whizzing back and forth until the other team slammed an across-the-court smash. Sarah dove for it and missed. *"Aaaah!"* she cried as she slid painfully into a three-point landing—leaving skid marks from her knees and elbow.

Of course, if this were a movie, she'd have clobbered the ball, come back from behind, and leapt over the net in victory. Unfortunately, it wasn't a movie. Instead it was "40-Love," "Game," "Match," and another major defeat for her team.

Slowly she got to her feet, snatched her towel, and marched toward the locker room in frustration. Tina was right behind her.

"Why didn't you let it go?" Tina snapped.

"What?"

"The ball—it was going out-of-bounds! Why didn't you let it go?"

"Because I thought it was in!" Sarah shot back. "My head was, like, four inches off the ground. Things aren't so clear with your nose that close to concrete," she growled. "Besides, if you hadn't given them a lob to smash back, I wouldn't have been in that position in the first place!"

"Gee, you know," Tina said, struggling to keep her cool, "I really thought we could take these guys."

"Well, we couldn't." Sarah's terse answer was delivered through clenched teeth. "But it would have helped if you had stayed close to the net like you were supposed to!"

With that, she sped up and burst through the locker-room door.

Usually there's nothing like a warm shower and a little locker-room chatter to cool things down. After all, Sarah was not only pretty, she was nice. The "Golden Rule" had been imprinted in her brain circuitry seventeen layers deep. Given time, it always went into effect. Well, almost always. . . .

"I never lose when I play by myself!" Sarah complained as she laced up her shoes. (Obviously the Golden Rule circuitry had shorted out somewhere.)

"And what's that supposed to mean?" Tina snapped as she whirled around to face her.

"All right, girls, that's enough!" the coach yelled from across the locker room. "Practice tomorrow at three o'clock sharp. We've got some work to do."

Neither Sarah nor Tina bothered to tune in to the announcement. Their eyes were still shooting sparks at each other.

"Are you saying you think you're better than I am?!" Tina glared.

"No—I mean—," Sarah stammered, beginning to remember her Golden Rule programming. Already she had started to regret her words. "Ohhh . . . forget it. Look . . . I'm sorry. It's just that . . . that . . ."

"That what?" Tina demanded.

"I just don't like . . . losing. Especially when it's all the time."

Tina heaved a sigh. "Well, who does?"

"Come on," Sarah said, slamming her locker door closed. "Let's get out of here and face the music."

"What music is that?" Tina asked while grabbing her duffel bag.

"The music everyone's making about us losing." Sarah sighed. "It's becoming the number-one hit of the school."

THREE
Cool Guys Wear Black

Once again Nick and Rex were back in the Martins' house, and they were redefining the fashion world. To be more exact, Rex was redefining Nick's wardrobe. After all, when it comes to cool dudedom, clothes don't make the man—they *are* the man.

"What about one of these?" Nick asked as he brought a fistful of shirts out of his closet.

"Dude," Rex pronounced, examining the stack from his kicked-back position on the bed, "you gotta stop shopping at Geeks-R-Us. There's not one designer label in here."

Nick tossed the shirts across the bed and plunged back into the closet searching for more.

"Look," Rex explained, "it's like this: Life is one big amusement park. All the cool people are inside, having a cool time. And all the uncool people are on the outside, trying to get tickets. Take a guess where you get tickets . . . ?"

Nick's head poked out of the closet. "I . . . I don't know."

"Junior high, dude." Rex rose from the bed and swaggered over to the mirror. "It's where the future begins, where you either get your ticket, like me—" He glided the comb smoothly through his hair. "Or . . ."

"You're left out?" Nick finished for him with a gulp. He looked at his latest handful of shirts and threw them disgustedly on top of the others.

"Exactly," Rex agreed. "But don't worry. I'm here to save you from terminal geekdom." Rex turned and glanced at the pile of shirts. "We may need to go malling."

"Huh?"

"Go to the mall," Rex translated. He circled around Nick, giving him the once-over. "Hmmm. Something's still missing," he mused, rubbing his chin. "I got it . . ." He pulled out a pair of shades and ceremoniously handed them to Nick. "They're yours, bro."

Nick couldn't believe his eyes. The "Rexster" was giving him his only pair of sunglasses? Incredible! Fantastic! Incredibly fantastic!

Well, not exactly . . .

Rex grinned as he drew out another pair of sunglasses and put them on. "I always keep a spare." The Ray•Ban duo turned together, like Siamese twins, and stared admiringly into the mirror.

"Whoa . . . definitely . . . non-geeky," Nick oozed.

"Totally cool," Rex echoed.

The next day a new dude invaded Eastfield Junior High. He was . . .

THE NICKSTER.

Totally malled, totally made over, totally hip—from his black T-shirt, to his black pants, to his black shoes—Nick looked a lot like a shadow wearing sunglasses. He strutted down the hallway as cool as an ice cube on a subzero day in the Arctic.

Philip did a double take when Mr. Ray•Ban drifted by. *Who was that masked man?* he wondered. Then, recognizing his old pal beneath the black wrappers, he started up the staircase after him. "Hey, Nick!" he shouted. "Nick, wait up!"

"Oh . . . hi," Nicholas mumbled as Philip finally caught up with him. Mr. Cool glanced about nervously, hoping nobody was watching. Oh, sure, Philip was a friend, but he was also a geek. And, as a recent refugee from geekdom, Nick could not afford to be seen hanging around with him.

"You want to go to the computer show on Saturday?" Philip asked in eager anticipation. "I heard they've got this really cool antivirus that uncrashes your hard drive and leaves a big happy face on your screen!"

"Uh . . . I don't know." Nick shrugged, wishing Philip would disappear before they reached the top of the stairs. "I'm not really into computers anymore." Actually, he still liked the little electronic wonders, but Rex had said they weren't cool, so, of course, they were out.

"You're not interested?" Philip asked, his expression starting to fall. Nick glanced away and said nothing. "Well, OK." Philip tried to shrug it off, but it was pretty obvious that Nick's rejection hurt the little guy.

Mr. Cool One pretended not to notice. Instead he mumbled a "Catch you later, dude" and started down the hall.

"'Dude'?" Philip coughed slightly on the word. He watched Nick saunter away, more than a little puzzled.

As Nick approached his locker he let out a sigh of relief. Ever since Rex had helped transform him to "cool," he'd been dreading the encounter with Philip, the All-School Loser. Now that it was over, Nicholas thought he'd handled it pretty well. Smooth and easy. No contamination.

Contamination! Nick paused and frowned slightly. He didn't exactly mean that Philip was some sort of impurity. Or did he?

Suddenly Rex appeared, dead ahead, surrounded by a couple of his clones and clonettes as they all headed down the hallway. Nick nodded to them and noticed somebody dangling from Rex's arm. This was not just any somebody. This somebody really had *some body.* She was the foxiest sample of femininity this side of sweet sixteen. Translation: She was hot. Or was it "cool"? (Nick hadn't entirely mastered the subtleties of "cool-ese" yet.)

"Lookin' buff, dude!" Rex said to Nick with an easy high five as they arrived. He tilted down his glasses to give Nick's outfit the once-over. "Nice kicks!"

"Thanks, dude," Nick returned proudly. He glanced shyly at the girl. "They're real leather!"

"What other kind is there?" Rex chuckled over his own wit before turning to his classy companion. "Babs Jenkins," he said, "meet my newest, uh . . . friend, Nick Martin."

Friend? He called me . . . friend! Nick thought. He felt like he'd been knighted or something.

"Do I, like, know you?" Babs asked in her best superstar wanna-be voice.

"Actually," Nick croaked, "I sit near you in Spanish."

"Oh . . . like, wow, I hadn't noticed." She lowered her

shades for a better look. "Bummer." Exactly who or what she meant by "bummer" was hard to tell, but it didn't matter to Nicholas—he was still blushing under her baby blues.

Just down the hall, near his own locker, Philip watched this little soap opera in amazement. Suddenly Renee appeared. "Hi, Philip!" she said as she opened her locker door. Philip said nothing; he was too busy staring. Puzzled by his silence, she turned to follow his eyes to Rex, Babs, and—Nicholas?

"Why's Nick hanging out with Ken and Barbie?" she quipped.

"Got me," Philip muttered.

"And when did he start dressing all in black? He looks like Batman."

Just then, who should appear beside them but the primo cool dude of them all—Derrick Cryder. He slung open his locker and shoved in a load of books.

Books? Derrick Cryder? If this had been last year, Philip and Renee would have passed out in amazement. But the former bully and all-around bad dude had undergone some heavy-duty spiritual renovation last Christmas. Nobody was exactly sure what had happened, but one thing had become clear: Derrick was no longer the Derrick Cryder they all had known and hated. Not since he and Nick had had their little Christmas Eve encounter . . . and got to talking about Jesus.

"Hey," he grunted to Renee and Philip. "What's with Martin?"

"That's what we'd like to know," Philip answered absently. Suddenly he noticed who he was talking to.

"Ahhh, oh, hi, Derrick." He knew Derrick had gone through some changes, but Philip didn't like to take chances. He still treated him with the utmost respect. After all, at one time, Philip had served as Derrick's personal punching bag.

Derrick didn't respond. He'd already seen enough. Without a word he slammed his locker and moved down the hall.

Meanwhile, back in Coolville, Nicholas and Rex also thought it was time to split. "So, Nick," Rex said with a glance back toward Philip and Renee, "you're going to bag that nimrod squad you usually hang out with and go to the Battle of the Bands with us, right?"

"Really?" Nick asked in astonishment. "Well, yeah . . . sure!"

"Hard to believe, huh?" Rex flashed him a grin. "Not too many kids can say they hang out with me." Then with a thumbs-up and chuckle he said, "Later, dude," and slinked on down the hall.

"Yeah . . . later." Nick gave a wave in the air, then quickly tucked his hands into his pockets. Cool dudes don't wave.

The bell rang and everyone scurried off in different directions. Everyone but Derrick. He had seen the rest of the "Too Cool to Be Real" show from down the hall. And he didn't much like the opening act.

FOUR
Who's a Wanna-Be?

Sarah was supposed to be working on her chemistry experiment, but the school paper was opened next to her Bunsen burner. And right there, smack in the center page, was the headline: "Girl's Tennis Tromped . . . *Again!*"

"Why can't they just keep quiet about it?" Sarah fumed. Then she spotted it: her photograph. It was from their last match, the one where she'd lunged for the ball and skidded across the asphalt. The picture caught her flying through the air, her legs twisted awkwardly, her arms flailing. It was a great picture, if you happened to be a Raggedy Ann doll tumbling out of control. But if you were a teenager of the female persuasion and worried about what others thought, it was time for some major embarrassment. It wasn't that Sarah was mortified, it's just that she knew plastic surgery was the only way to avoid total humiliation.

"All right . . ." Her chemistry teacher's voice startled her. "What kind of reaction did you get when you added the potassium chlorate to the substance in the flask?"

Sarah scrambled to catch up. She scooted the school paper aside and fumbled through the chemical jars. In front of her were two filled flasks and a small cup holding some-

175

thing powdery. She rubbed her forehead trying to think. She knew that the powder was the potassium stuff, but . . .

Oh, help! she thought. *Which flask am I supposed to pour it into?*

She had two options: she could "Eeny, meeny, miny, mo" between the two flasks, or she could admit she wasn't listening and ask for help. But since she'd just seen her photo and wasn't in the mood for any more humiliation, she gave a heavy sigh and "Eeny, meeny, miny, moed" it. She picked up the potassium and poured it into the "Mo" flask.

Suddenly it became clear that "Miny" would have been the better move. There was a bright flash accompanied by a small but very impressive *KA-BOOOOOOOOOOOM!!*

"Aughhh!" Sarah screamed, leaping backward off her stool. She crashed into the student behind her, causing him to sprawl into his own experiment, sending his flasks and beakers crashing to the ground.

It wasn't exactly a nuclear meltdown, but it was close enough. There was something about the way the fireball in Sarah's flask kept burning and the nearby students kept running and screaming that kind of got everyone's attention.

"What's going on there?" the teacher shouted. *"Sarah!?"*

He raced to her side and swept the fireball flask into the sink, then turned on the water full blast. Finally, when the fire was out, he turned to Sarah. His look could have burned through steel.

Sarah was not intimidated. Her response was clear and to the point: "Uh . . . I . . . that is to say . . . uh . . ."

Several minutes later, Sarah was on her hands and

knees wiping up the floor. All the other students had gone to lunch. Her teacher loomed above her like a thundercloud. A very angry thundercloud.

Finally she rose to her feet, looking more than a little sorrowful. "Mr. Murchison, I'm so sorry. I . . . I . . ."

"We'll talk about it Monday," he said as he headed for the door. "If you don't mind, I'll try to enjoy the last twenty minutes of my lunch break. Just hang up the rags in the cabinet and pull the door shut when you leave." With that he was gone.

Sarah pulled the rubber gloves up higher on her arms as she dropped back to her knees to resume wiping up the spill. *What a day*, she thought. *First my picture in the paper, then this mess . . . what else could go wrong?*

"Hi, Sarah."

She looked up, startled. For a moment, the sweat in her eyes fogged her vision. She blinked. Morgan Jefferson! It couldn't be! She blinked again . . . and he was still there. No big deal, of course, except that he just happened to be Eastfield High's star quarterback and number-one junior class heartthrob!

She quickly sat up, wiping her face with her sleeve. What lousy timing! Here she was with this awesome hunk of teenage maledom and what was she doing? Playing Cinderella . . . and without the glass slipper!

"Oh, hi," she said, trying somehow to look a little dignified.

"I felt kind of bad, leaving you here all alone," he said. "After all, some of the mess was mine."

"Yours?" Sarah asked, startled.

"Well, yeah. If you remember, I was the guy behind you when the fireworks started."

"That was you I bumped into?" Suddenly Sarah felt even more embarrassed. "It wasn't your fault," she stammered. "I was the klutz who made you knock all your stuff over."

"True," he laughed. "If it had been football, you'd have been called for clipping." He knelt down beside her and took one of her rags. "But I'm from the old school that says a guy never lets a girl take the rap by herself."

"Well . . . thanks," she said, barely able to find her voice. She couldn't believe it. Here he was, Morgan Jefferson, All-School Everything, scrubbing right alongside her.

"Don't tell my mom I did this," he said with a grin. "The next thing you know, she'll be having me scrub the kitchen floor on a regular basis."

"I promise." Sarah laughed. Then after a moment she said, "Now all I have to do is find some way to salvage my chemistry grade."

"You?" Morgan asked with a chuckle. "The class brain?"

"What do you mean 'class brain'?" she shot back, smiling. "You're the one who's always got the answers."

"Just luck," he said with a shrug, "and the fact that I always look over your shoulder to get them." He laughed as she gave him an astonished, wide-eyed look.

Sarah had always felt shy around Morgan. Eastfield High's football team was the best they'd been in years, and everybody said it was because of him. Then there was the little matter of him being the best-looking and nicest boy in school. Some of the girls had told Sarah they'd seen him looking at her, but she knew better. Or at least, she thought she did. After all, Morgan could have his pick of any girl in Eastfield—or of the whole state, for that matter.

Yet, here they were. What had started out so wrong was suddenly starting to look like something so right. It *was* Cinderella time, and she didn't even need the glass slipper.

"What's this?" Morgan asked, flipping over Sarah's waterlogged school paper, which happened to be on the floor beside him. "So what's in the news today? Ah yes, the tennis team."

Sarah winced. If he read any further, he'd see her name. If he looked at the picture he'd recognize her face. She had to do something fast. Quickly she rose from the floor and began picking up all the trash. "We'd better hurry or we'll completely miss lunch," she said as she tried to snatch the paper from his hands.

No luck. Morgan hung on.

"Zero and seven!" He whistled as he continued to scan the article. "What a bunch of losers. They just can't get it together, can they?"

Sarah looked frantically about. "Uh, I . . . I'm sure th-they're doing the best they—" Then she saw it: a small beaker of water on the workbench just above Morgan and the paper. She swallowed hard—she had no other choice. She reached over to the beaker and deliberately knocked it off the workbench.

"Hey!" Morgan yelled as the water spilled across the article and Sarah's picture.

"Sorry," she said as she snatched the soggy paper from his hands. "This just doesn't seem to be my day." She gave a silent sigh of relief as she crossed over and dumped the wadded-up paper into the trash. Of course, she couldn't keep this up forever. Somebody was bound to become suspicious if she kept running around ripping papers out of everybody's hands. For now, though, it was the only plan she had.

Morgan picked up their rags and hung them on the rack in the cabinet. "Man, I hate to lose," he said, not giving up the subject.

"Me, too," Sarah agreed softly. She took off her gloves and laid them on the counter, but before she could pick up her books Morgan scooped them into his hands and nodded toward the door.

"After you."

"Thanks." Sarah walked ahead of him, beaming like a searchlight as they headed into the hall.

"I tell you," he continued, "if our football team was doing that badly I couldn't even show my face in the school."

Sarah swallowed hard. She looked down, praying none of the passing students would notice her while they headed down the hall.

Back in junior-high land, Nick was showing his face everywhere. Only it was his new-and-not-so-improved face. The last class of the day was over when he ran into Renee near his locker.

"So, what's with the new look?" Renee asked as she approached.

Since cool guys don't study, Nick tossed his books into his locker. "What's wrong?" he shot back. "Too cool for you?"

"No . . ." His attitude caught Renee a little off guard. "It's fine. It's just . . . different."

"Well, I wouldn't expect *you* to like it."

"Soooooorryyy!" Renee flung back at him angrily. Then, without another word, she stomped over to her own locker. If he wanted to be a jerk, let him be a jerk—but he'd have to do it with somebody else.

Nicholas knew his reaction might have been a little overkill, but he was only trying to better himself, to be somebody. What was wrong with that? Hey! You've got to make some sacrifices if you want to succeed.

At that moment Jordan, the new friend on the block, took a running slide up to his locker, which was between Nick's and Renee's. Besides being a super jock (complete with letter jacket and the accompanying biceps), Jordan was a pretty good artist.

"Yo, Nick. Yo, Renee." He tossed a football into the air before trying to remember his combination.

Still burning, Renee gave him a halfhearted nod as she threw open her locker with a loud bang.

Nick didn't even give him that much of a greeting.

Having no idea he had just stepped into the middle of World War III, Jordan continued, "Hey Nick, ever since you showed me that 3-D thing, my drawings are really popping!"

Nick said nothing so Jordan rattled on. "Fact is, I'm thinkin' about havin' a double career: NFL quarterback and computer graphics genius!"

"That's cool," Nick said, in his best ho-hum manner.

Still clueless about the war, Jordan turned to Renee. "Hey, Renee, you guys talked about the Battle of the Bands yet? We all gonna go together or what?"

Renee brightened at the thought. "Sounds great to me."

181

Then she added warily, "But you better check with Mr. Cool there."

Jordan turned to Nick. "How 'bout it, Nicholas?"

"Uh . . ." Nick seemed at a loss for words. It was major decision time. If he was going to make a move away from these losers, it was now or never. Finally he mumbled. "No, uh, no thanks."

Renee tried her best to hide the hurt crossing her face, but she didn't do too well. That was OK, though, since Nick wouldn't have noticed anyway. He was staring at Rex and Babs, who were making a grand entrance down the stairs. With them was a new member of the herd. She was a beauty straight out of a Jordache commercial: tall, blonde, and green-eyed. She was definitely "Beverly Hills 90210" material. In short, she was . . .

"Wow!"

Nobody heard him say it, but Nick couldn't help letting that little exclamation slip from his lips.

Rex and his Barbie clones strode past Jordan and Renee as if they were hallway mannequins. But they did manage to stop in front of Nick.

"Dude," Rex said as he nodded toward the new girl. "This is Jessica. She's gonna hang with us at the Battle."

"Cool," Nick managed to croak through a mouth that had suddenly turned as dry as the Sahara. He caught Renee shooting him a pained look, so he shifted his face from her view.

"What're we doing slumming around here?" Rex said as he glanced over to Jordan and Renee. He flashed them his best put-down look, a Rex speciality. "Let's go over to my place and chill," he said.

"Fer sure," Babs and Jessica recited in perfect, mindless unison. Renee thought they sounded like electronic dolls. Given the chance, she was sure she could short-circuit their little wires in two seconds flat—maybe less.

"That sounds cool!" Nick answered. Again he almost caught Renee's eye, and again he quickly shifted his line of vision. When you're playing Benedict Arnold, one thing you don't want is to check in with Betsy Ross.

Rex put his arm around Nick and pulled him along the hallway. "A little advice, Nickster . . ." He made sure he spoke loud enough so Renee and Jordan could hear. "When you're cool, everyone else is a wanna-be . . . very uncool to hang out with wanna-bes."

Renee stared after them in disbelief. "'Wanna-bes'?"

"Wanna-be what?" Jordan asked, once again missing the point by a mile.

Renee, on the other hand, got the point. And it landed right in her gut. OK, so maybe she wasn't going to win Miss Popularity, or maybe she needed a few more curves in a few more places, but at least she had more than golden curls and hot air beneath a designer hat. So how could her good buddy, Nicholas Martin, suddenly treat her so badly?

Renee wasn't the only one puzzled by Nick's little performance.

Derrick Cryder leaned against the wall, gnawing on a toothpick. He had just seen the second act of this little show, and he didn't like it any better than the first.

Obviously, something had to be done. . . .

FIVE
So Long, McGee

My spaceship touched down on the planet Gobbley-Goop with a low whine and a loud KER-SPLAT! The whine came from my turbo thrusters, but the KER-SPLAT had me completely baffled . . . until I hopped out of the capsule and sank up to my aroma-free armpits in banana cream filling.

Immediately I did what any peace ambassador and part-time junk food junkie would do: I ate like a pig!

True, I was sent by the Federation of Planets to establish peace on this war-torn world—but we are talking about banana cream pies here . . . with golden graham cracker crusts!

Still, my feeding frenzy was short-lived.

"Look out, Mr. Ambassador!"

I spun around just in time to see half a dozen lemon meringue pies flying at me. I had two choices:

A. Duck.
B. Leap up and chow down as many of those palatable projectiles as possible.

Being the health-conscious hero that I am, I chose to duck instead of leap (mostly 'cause my leaper was a bit overloaded from all those banana creams I'd been putting down). "What's going on?" I screamed as the delectable delicacies sailed over my head.

"It's the Pie-droids!" a young man to my left screamed. "They're attacking us with everything they've got!" From the mashed potatoes and carrots smeared across his face, I immediately knew he was a member of that much-loved and well-respected race, the Vegetable-flingers. Much loved by everyone but the Pie-droids, that is.

For centuries the Pie-droids and Vegetable-flingers had been at war; for generations their children had wakened to the vicious sound of flying vegetables and plummeting pies. And now here I was, McGee the Marvelous, Ambassador of Goodwill, Perpetrator of Peace (and a dropout of Weight Watchers), trying to restore order.

That was the good news. The bad news was I was standing directly between the two warring armies.

"Incoming!" a Pie-droid to my right yelled. Suddenly ten tablespoons of corn and four heads of overcooked broccoli exploded at my feet.

As the vegetables cascaded around me I jumped to my left foot, then my right, then my left again. . . . I looked like some crazy tap dancer. So I grabbed the cane and top hat I keep in my briefcase just for such occasions and began an impressive song-and-dance routine of "Old Folks at Home." Stephen C. Foster couldn't have done it better himself.

> "Way down upon de Swanee Ribber,
> Far, far away . . ."

"Stop it!" the Pie-droids screamed.

> "Dere's wha my heart is turning ebber,
> Dere's wha de old folks stay . . ."

"*Make him quit!*" *the Vegetable-flingers cried. But nothing would stop these talented tootsies or silence my sensational singing:*

> "All up and down de whole creation
> Sadly I roam,
> Still longing for de old plantation,
> And for de old folks at home!"

The vegetables came harder and faster.
So did the pies.
It was like a giant dessert and salad bar . . . all you can eat, all at once, all raining down on top of me. But I wasn't worried. How could I be? I'm the hero of this story. Besides, it was all part of my plan. It was why I was chosen in the first place. I'll explain more as soon as I'm done with the chorus. All together now:

> "All de world am sad and dreary,
> Da-da-da-da-deee . . ."

"Da-da-dee's" are always good when you forget the words. And thanks to all the banging my beanie was getting from the zinging zucchini and pelting pies, my memory—along with the rest of my brain—was going fast. Still, being the fearless hero I am, I pressed on.
"Please!" they cried, holding their ears in agony. "Please stop."
But I just kept singing and dancing. "Second chorus!" I shouted. "Everybody join in if you know the words."

"All right! All right!" they cried, dropping to their knees, tears streaming down their cheeks. "We'll do anything you say!"

"Anything?" I beamed, still tapping the paint off my cartoon tootsies.

"Anything," they shouted back.

"You'll stop this senseless war?"

They hesitated.

I sang louder.

"All right, all right!" they screamed. "We'll stop fighting. Just—just quit that awful noise!"

I came to a stop. Both sides broke into applause—then a standing ovation. (I knew I was good, but not that good.)

Over the next few days, we began the delicate phase of disarmament. But we didn't destroy the weapons. No sir. Not the way worldwide hunger is spreading. Instead the Veggie-flingers donated their wholesome goodies to hundreds of junk food rehab centers. They figured junk food addicts from around the country would come in and trade their chips and candies for broccoli and cauliflower. (Yeah, right. Like these people are in touch with reality. . . .)

"But what about the pies?" the Veggie-flingers asked suspiciously. "If we give up our vegetables, what are the Pie-droids willing to do with their pies?"

I flashed them my famous ambassador smile. "Trust me."

The following day my spacecraft was ready to leave for home. It was a little tricky getting off the ground with all the deep-dish apples, lemon meringues, and coconut creams stored on board, but I was willing to take the risk if it meant bringing permanent peace to this troubled world.

With a mighty K-WOOOOSH! I took off. Now it was just

me and the thousands of tons of sugar-saturated, fabulously fruity, candy-coated calories. But that's OK, somebody had to make the sacrifice. It's a tough job (burp) but somebody's gotta (belch) do it. (Ahhh . . .)

Now I could settle back and enjoy the fact that, once again, a mightily magnificent job was masterminded by the marvelous—

Whoa!

Suddenly my spaceship dissolved, the pies vanished, and I was back on the sketch pad, where I had just enjoyed this little fantasy. As I wiped the make-believe crumbs from my mouth, my beautiful baby blues caught a glimpse of Nick outside the window. Good timing! By the looks of things I could use some touch-up paint on my tap-dancing tootsies—not to mention a little tummy tuck around the ol' pie disposal unit. (Good thing he'd sketched me in erasable pencil.)

The best I figured—and believe me, nothing's finer than my fancy figuring (unless, of course, you're talking dill pickles smothered in chocolate sauce, one of my all-time favorite munchies)—ol' Nick had been hanging out with Rex the Wreck again. Personally, I'd like to lock old Rexy boy in a room and throw away the room! Right now, though, it looked like I had a more important mission than ridding the world of Rex the Mess. From the looks of my buddy, I knew it was time to launch "Operation Save Nick from Himself."

A minute later Nicholas burst into his room like a kid looking for eggs on Easter. He'd just gotten a little chocolate stain on his white T-shirt, but the way he was panicking you'd think they'd just outlawed Nintendo.

"Mo-o-o-o-om!" he screamed as he rushed to the mirror and anxiously rubbed at the tiny stain with his washrag.

Mom was right behind him. "You know, honey, tooth-paste and bleach will take that stain right out." She reached for his shirt. "Just take this off and I'll—"

But Nicholas yanked away. "I can take care of it myself, Mom!" That kind of behavior and lip would have normally gotten Nick grounded for life, but his mom was so surprised, she just stared at her obnoxious offspring. "Well . . . OK." She headed back to the door, then her face lit up like a Christmas tree. "Oh, Nick," she said, spinning back to him. "Guess what?"

Nick sighed. Somehow he figured he'd know "what" whether he guessed it or not. He was right.

"Your dad doesn't know it yet, but I'm getting out his old saxophone. They're going to ask him to do a little jam session at the Battle of the Bands. Won't that be . . . cool?" Her voice trailed off as she looked for a reaction, maybe even a grin.

Nick gave her nothing, except for a roll of the eyes and a little groan. "Oh, yeah, cool—like being hit in the head with a glacier."

Once again Mom wasn't exactly sure what to think about this new Nick, so she just gave him a weak smile and headed out the door.

Nick turned his attention back to the stain. "Good job," he sighed as he kept rubbing at it. "I might as well have just drooled on myself!"

Well, it was time to set the kid straight. Time to share my intelligently insightful intellect. I hopped off the sketch pad and onto the drawing table.

190

"Come on, Nick," I said. "That's only a plain white T-shirt, more commonly known as underwear!"

"McGeeeee," Nick returned impatiently, "it's the only cool shirt I have!"

"Hey! What about that other one—the one that says 'Cartoons are our friends'?"

"Get real, McGee. It might as well say, 'I'm a geek and proud of it.'"

I couldn't believe my ears. "You used to love that shirt!" I cried.

"That was before," Nick said as he whirled away from the mirror.

"Before what?" I demanded.

He just shrugged.

"You mean, before you got . . . cool?" I was really beginning to hate that word.

"Well . . . yeah," Nick answered. Before I knew it he had stalked into the closet and started rummaging through his clothes. "There's nothing here!" he whined. "Nothing at all!"

I began pacing back and forth on the art table. "Kid, you're out of control!" I called. "That 'hair-for-brains' Rexster has made you somebody else! You're bagging on your family and your friends and—"

"Hang it up, McGee!" Nick's voice echoed from inside the closet. Finally he appeared in the doorway, his finger pointing accusingly at me. "Who gave you the right to tell me what to do?"

"Nobody's telling you—"

"I'm the one who created you!"

"Well, yeah, but—"

"Out of nothing!"

"Sure, but—"

"Remember??"

I was lucky to get a word in edgewise . . . or sideways . . . or on its head. "But I'm your best friend," I fired back. "I have privileges!"

Nick fidgeted uncomfortably. I waited.

He leaned against the door and shoved his hands into his pockets. "I'm not so sure of that anymore . . . ," he said, not looking at me.

"WHAT?!" I couldn't believe my ears. I stuck my finger into them and gave a good shake. Nothing came out but your usual killer moths, vampire bats, and flying UFOs. (I tell you, I've got to stop watching those late-night TV movies.)

"Draw me some Q-Tips," I continued. "I thought I heard you say . . . we're not friends anymore."

"That's right," Nick fired back. "Drawing cartoons is uncool for a guy my age! Cartoons are for kids!"

It was like he'd punched me in the gut. I couldn't catch my breath. If Nicky quit drawing me—if we quit being friends—it would be curtains, it would mean "Bye-bye McGee." And we ain't talkin' vacation to Disneyland. We're talking your basic "So long," "I'm history," "No more clever comebacks and irresistible insights." In short, I'd become nothing but another drawing on another piece of paper.

"Say it ain't so, kid!" I cried. "Say it ain't so!"

I waited for him to break into his world-famous grin and tell me it was all just a bad joke. Instead, Nick slowly turned his back on me.

And then he said it.

"Just go away. Leave me alone, McGee."

My colors started to fade.

"Nicholas . . ." I tried not to let the hurt come out in my voice. But my incredible wit began to grow witless, my keen intellect began to grow dim, and I started to panic.

"Nicholas . . . ?"

But my little buddy wouldn't turn to help. Any minute the worst of all worsts would happen. I, the magnificently marvelous McGee would become . . . gulp! . . . boring. After that . . . well, after that there was nothing left but cartoon oblivion.

"Nicholas!"

Suddenly my feet started moving. Before I knew it I was heading for the drawing pad. I couldn't help myself. Something was pulling me toward it. As I stepped onto the paper glanced at my hands. They were barely visible. Everything about me was fading.

I tried to think of something clever to say, but the cleverness was gone. My brain was going to sleep. I could no longer think.

I was lying down on the pad now. I tried to sit up, but I no longer had the energy to move. I was stuck to the paper for good. With my last ounce of energy I turned my head toward the boy standing across the room. I thought I knew him, but I wasn't sure. I wanted to call out his name, but I could no longer remember it.

And then . . .

There was nothing.

SIX
Too Cool to Be Real

"C'mon, Jamie, move it!" Sarah yelled up the stairs. "You're gonna make us late!"

"All right, all right," Jamie's voice echoed from above.

"I'm supposed to meet Tina and a couple of the girls from the team at 4:00," Sarah complained. "If you want to tag along that's OK, but not if you're going to make me late."

"All right, all right," Jamie repeated as she scrambled down the steps. On her head was a bright, neon pink bicycle helmet.

"What are you doing with that?" Sarah demanded.

"It's what I wear when you drive."

"Cute," Sarah said scornfully. "Now let's get going. You know how hard it is to find parking at the mall this time of day."

Half an hour later, Sarah and Jamie rushed through the mall toward Yogurt Yums, the Saturday afternoon gathering place for the Eastfield High School crowd. Sarah spotted Tina and a couple of other girls from the tennis team sitting at one of the tables, waiting for her. They were putting down a couple of scoops of the no-fat, no-cholesterol, no-taste treat. Sarah raised her hand and started to call to them when suddenly . . .

She heard a giggle. Out of the corner of her eye she caught a couple of cheerleaders laughing with some football jocks. No biggie. A typical, everyday sight: airheads with bicep-brains. Except for one small difference.

One of the jocks was Morgan Jefferson!

"Ohhh, not now!" Sarah groaned as she reached out to grab Jamie.

"Ow!" Jamie cried as she was yanked to an abrupt stop. "What are you trying to do, give me whiplash?"

Sarah didn't have time to explain. In spite of the school paper's photo, she had managed to keep her identity as a tennis player a secret from Morgan. In fact, things were going really well between the two of them . . . but it could all end, right this moment, if he discovered she was a part of the loser crowd. She didn't have time to explain any of that; she just had time to do something drastic—like get out of there, fast!

She spun Jamie around and started toward the nearest exit, then she heard:

"Hey, Sarah!" It was Morgan. He'd spotted her and now, all smiles and waves, he started toward her. Sarah gave him a nervous smile and a halfhearted wave. She glanced quickly toward Tina. It was just as she feared. Tina had heard Sarah's name and was looking around. Bingo! Their eyes connected. Sarah looked away as if she hadn't seen her. But it was too late, and they both knew it.

She looked back to Morgan. He was nearly there.

"Hi!" He grinned. "Blown up any more schools lately?"

Sarah laughed uncomfortably as she threw another

look to Tina. Great, just great. Tina and her tennis friends were rising to their feet. Sarah knew what was coming next.

"You going to the game Friday night?" Morgan asked.

But Sarah didn't hear. She was too busy praying that the ground would open up and swallow her whole.

"Sarah?" he repeated.

"Huh?"

"Can you make it to our game Friday?"

"Well, uh, I . . ." She thought she sounded like a babbling fool. She was right. As Tina and the team started toward her, she wondered if this was what the captain of the *Titanic* felt when he saw the iceberg coming.

"I was wondering," Morgan continued, "if you'd—"

"Uh . . . I have to go now," Sarah interrupted. "Come on Jamie." She gave Jamie another yank and started toward the exit. Any exit.

"Ow!" Jamie cried, yanking her hand out of Sarah's grip and planting her feet like a stubborn mule.

Morgan tried again. "I . . . was just wondering if you'd like to go out for a Coke or something after the game?"

"Uh . . ."

"Sarah?" Tina called out, a little puzzled, as she and the team approached.

"Uh . . ."

"Sarah??" They were practically there!

And then, just to make things worse, one of the cheerleaders, Mary Lynn, the class barracuda, suddenly appeared next to Morgan. She put her hand on his shoulder and flashed Sarah a smile so sugarcoated it would make your teeth rot. "Hey, Morgan," she giggled. "I didn't know you knew our little tennis-team captain."

Sarah gulped. She wasn't sure where to look. To Morgan? Or her friends? But Mary Lynn wasn't finished yet. She leaned a fist on her cocked hip. "So tell me, Sarah, you girls planning on winning any matches this year?"

"Hey, Sarah." Tina gave her a put-out look as she arrived. She could tell Sarah was embarrassed, and she had a sneaky feeling she knew the reason.

"Well, speak of the devil," Mary Lynn gloated. "If it isn't the rest of the losers."

Sarah tried to speak, but nothing came out. She wanted to say it was all a terrible mistake, that there was a girl who looked just like her on the tennis team. She wanted to deny that she ever knew Tina. She wanted to race right out and buy Mary Lynn a ticket to Mars for Christmas. But nothing happened. She just stood there, her face on fire.

"I . . ." She turned to Morgan. "I'll see you in chemistry."

With that she turned and left, dragging the protesting Jamie all the way.

Mary Lynn looked on in satisfaction.

Morgan watched in confusion.

And Tina? She stood there, hurt in her eyes, feeling the pain that only comes when your best friend stabs you in the back.

By the night of "The Battle of the Bands," Nicholas had changed everything: his clothes, his friends, his room. Gone were all his neat inventions. Gone were all his

McGee drawings. In fact, you had to look hard just to find his drawing table. Now it was hidden under a stack of heavy metal CDs, which, of course, were Rex's. Nick's allowance (not to mention his mom and dad) would never let him start a collection of "that kind of music."

Nick was at his favorite spot, in front of the mirror, when there was a knock on the door.

"Come in," he called as he splashed on some cologne.

Mom and Dad entered. Nick nearly dropped the cologne bottle when he saw them. They were decked out, from head to toe, in sixties getups. Dad wore bell-bottom jeans, a checkered shirt, and a flowered vest. Then, of course, there was the hair combed straight down over the forehead. And what "Beatles look" would be complete without John Lennon glasses?

But as bad as Dad looked, Mom looked worse. First there was the neon green miniskirt, then the love beads—and let's not forget those ever-white and ever-popular go-go boots!

"How do we look?" Mom asked with a broad grin.

Nick suppressed a gag. "This is a joke, right? Nobody's wearing costumes. You're not really gonna go like that, are you?" (Maybe Rex was right—maybe his parents really *were* from another universe.)

"Of course we are," Mom said. "Your principal thought it would be fun if we dressed up in a sixties look."

"Yeah." Nick fumbled for the words. "But couldn't you just wear a . . . a peace sign or something?"

Dad put his arm around Nicholas's shoulder. "What's the matter, Son?" he chuckled. "Don't wanna be seen with half the members of the Mamas and Papas?"

The situation called for drastic action. Unfortunately Nick didn't have a clue what that would be. Changing his name and plastic surgery came to mind, but none of those could be done in the next hour or so. Well, at least there was one way out.

"Now that you mention it, Dad, I'm gonna walk over there with my friends."

"Oh, Nick," Mom said, a little disappointed, "I thought we'd be going as a family."

Nicholas plopped down on his bed, avoiding their eyes. "I see you guys all the time," he whined. "I'd rather go with my friends."

"We understand that," Dad said as he sat next to him. "We just assumed that tonight, since your mom and I have been asked to be hosts—"

Nick's patience broke. "That's another thing!" he blurted out as he jumped up from the bed. "Why do they have to make such a big deal of this twenty-five-year thing anyway?" He paced to the other side of the room. "Come Monday, every kid in school is gonna be laughing at me and saying, 'There goes Nick, son of the world's oldest living teenyboppers.'"

Silence fell over the room. Mom and Dad exchanged worried glances. Worried and hurt. Finally Dad spoke up. "Are you . . . embarrassed by us, Son?"

Nick paced faster. "It . . . it's just not cool to have your parents show up at the biggest event of the year! And to show up like—like this. . . . It's, like, the ultimate embarrassment!"

Again Mom and Dad traded looks. Nick had never said he was embarrassed by them before. This was supposed to be fun—a joke. Everybody was supposed to laugh. But right now, laughing was the last thing any of them had on their minds.

At last Dad gave a deep sigh and walked over to Nick. "We've always said there are some decisions we're gonna have to let you make on your own." He placed a hand gently on his son's shoulder. "If you don't want to go with us, I guess it's your choice."

Mom and Dad turned and walked toward the door. They looked back one last time. Dad tried to smile as he said, "We'll do our best to stay out of your way tonight, Son."

There was a knot in Nick's chest the size of a tennis ball. A part of him wanted to say something—to tell them it was OK and he would be proud of whatever they did. But that part had gotten awfully small—and it was growing smaller by the minute.

Instead, he swallowed hard and said nothing.

SEVEN
Getting Real

Cars surged through the parking lot like ants with head-lights. Squadrons of junior highers piled out of the doors and swarmed up the steps, passing beneath a banner that read "25th Annual Battle of the Bands."

Tonight was the night. The "battle" was on, and Eastfield Junior High gymnasium was the war zone. Inside, the hallway was swarming with teens and teachers. Everyone milled about or lined up at the tables to buy tickets.

Besides the millers and the liners, there were the leaners. Among them, Rex and Nick. They had the best leaning spot in the hall. Anybody coming through the doors had to see them: shades down, decked out in the coolest duds, the hottest chicks dangling from their arms—they couldn't be missed. Any second they expected the Webster folks to show up, take their picture, and put it in the dictionary under the new and improved definition of "cool."

Usually people who came through the doors wouldn't even rate a nod from this hip foursome. But Rex was feeling particularly generous this evening. Occasionally he would actually tip his shades when a fellow brother of coolness passed.

"Rex," the beautiful Babs squealed, "you are, like, so *très* cool!"

Though he had no idea what she meant, Rex grunted in agreement. After all she'd used the word *cool* so it must be good.

"So, dude," Nick asked as he gave an awkward thumbs-up to another cool passerby. "When are we, like, going in?"

"Chill, dude," Rex answered with a shrug. "We'll get around to it. Meantime, there's only one thing I wanna do. . . ."

"What's that?"

"Be seen, bud. Be seen. It's what makes life cool."

Babs and Jessica giggled with delight at Rex's deep insight. Just then a particular group of uncool teens walked by. Among them were Renee and Jordan. Nick's eyes followed Renee. She looked kind of nice . . . sweet . . . even pretty. Unfortunately nice, sweet, and pretty don't qualify as "cool."

"Hi, Nick," she said with a sad smile as she passed. Nick managed a little nod.

"Like . . . who was that?" Babs asked with a sarcastic laugh. "Little Miss Muffet?" Rex and Jessica snickered with her as they glanced at Nick.

Nicholas swallowed hard. "A friend," he said, forcing his own kind of half laugh.

"You mean, *former* friend," Rex corrected.

Nick hesitated, then nodded. He wasn't sure why, but he was beginning to get a headache. Maybe it was the shades. Maybe it was all this work of being cool. Or maybe it was something else. . . .

Before Nick had time to give it any more thought, Rex spotted somebody down at the far end of the hall. "Watch this," he said with an evil grin. He pulled out a marker from his coat and crossed over to the row of lockers.

Nicholas looked down the hallway to see who Rex had spotted. It was Philip. When Nick looked back, Rex had just finished writing the word *Geek* across Philip's locker. He stuffed the pen back into his pocket and quickly returned to his leaning position against the wall.

All eyes watched as Philip approached. Babs and Jessica started snickering. Then Philip spotted his locker.

The snickers grew louder.

Philip looked up. There was no missing the hurt in his eyes as he looked to Rex, then Babs, then Jessica, and finally . . . to Nicholas.

Nick looked down. He felt his jaw tighten. That tennis ball knot returned to his chest—only now it felt as big as a basketball.

Philip started to speak—he wanted to say something to his old buddy, but nothing came. Instead, he just blinked back the moisture filling his eyes, lowered his own head, and walked past without a word.

The basketball had risen to Nick's throat. He tried to swallow it back, but with little success.

"Come on, let's go in," Babs pleaded as she tugged at Rex's arm. "I spent, like, a whole month's allowance on this outfit. I wanna show it off!"

"Yeah, sure, it's cool," Rex agreed, giving her a quick

squeeze. "Come on." He signaled for Nick and Jessica to follow.

Nicholas turned toward the ticket table, but Rex immediately grabbed him by the collar. "Not that way, dude," he scorned. "That's the entrance for people who have to buy tickets."

"But . . ." Nick looked confused. "Don't we have to buy tickets?"

"No way, bro!" Rex chuckled as he glanced around for onlookers. Then, quickly, he herded Nick and the girls down a side hallway. "You're with me, remember?"

"Oh yeah," Nick muttered with a worried half smile. "Cool . . ." Nicholas's headache was getting worse. So was that basketball in his stomach or in his throat or wherever it was. Since when was ripping off the school and not paying your way "cool"?

As they ambled down the hallway, Nick kept glancing over his shoulder until Rex grabbed him and dragged him down a flight of stairs. As they descended the steps Nicholas had the distinct feeling he was sinking lower and lower—in more ways than one.

Moments later the four party-crashers appeared in the gym behind the bleachers. Rex strutted into the open like he had just outfoxed the CIA, FBI, and Agatha Christie all at the same time. Nick, on the other hand, sort of backed in with his head down. It had been a long time since he'd felt so rotten. He glanced around, and his eyes widened.

Either the gymnasium was really decorated or they were caught in some "Star Trek" time warp. The whole gym looked like a hangout from the late sixties, complete with surfboards, cutout palm trees, and a cardboard '68 Corvette convertible.

"Prehistoric, dude," Rex whispered.

Much to Nick's relief, nobody seemed to notice their back alley entrance. Nobody, that is, except Derrick. He was leaning against a wall doing his usual toothpick-chewing routine when he saw them come in. He knew Rex, so he wasn't surprised to see him make a thief's entrance. But when he saw Nick following, Derrick threw down his toothpick in disgust.

As the Cool-R-Us troop climbed up on the bleachers to sit, Mrs. Pryce stepped to the microphone. A ripple of chuckles wafted through the crowd when they saw her outfit. It probably had something to do with the yellow glow-in-the-dark miniskirt she wore.

"Testing . . . ah, hum . . . testing . . ."

WAAAAIIIIINGGGGGGGGGG!

That, of course, was feedback. After several seconds and lots of knob turning, the earsplitting sound finally faded.

Mrs. Pryce stepped back up to the microphone. "In a few minutes," she said, "we'll be ready to start our Endless Summer Battle of the Bands. I guarantee you, it will be very . . . groovy." She chuckled at her humor. Everyone else groaned. Everyone, that is, except Babs and Jessica. They were too busy critiquing the fashion scene to pay attention.

"Did you see what Sherry Nunnally is wearing?" Babs asked. "Don't you just want to gag?"

Jessica, whose vocabulary was usually limited to "oh my gosh" and "cool," managed to squeeze out a few giggles in agreement.

"Ouuu," Babs said, pointing across the room, "check out the Neanderthals!"

Nicholas's eyes followed her finger. He wished they hadn't. One of her ultramanicured, superlong, hot-red-polish-with-a-white-swirl-in-the-middle-of-the-nail fingers was jabbing right at his mom and dad. They were crossing toward Mrs. Pryce and yucking it up with some of the kids.

Before Nick could answer, Babs changed the subject again. "Nobody's seeing my outfit up here," she complained. "Can't we go mingle now?"

"Not if you wanna be cool," Rex answered. "When you're cool, you find some out-of-the-way place like this and let the minglers come to you."

Suddenly a firm hand gripped Nick's shoulder. He whipped around to see Derrick Cryder standing directly over him. Rex saw him, too. Immediately he ceased being the King of Cool. "Uh . . . h-hi, Derrick!" he stuttered.

Derrick grunted a nod. Then motioned to Nick. "The squid here and I need a little talk."

"Sure, Derrick," Rex said with an eager nod. "Whatever you say." He started to rise until Derrick flashed him a frown.

"Just the Nick . . . in private."

"Oh . . . yeah . . . sure . . ." Rex sat back down, looking a little deflated.

Nicholas glanced about as he rose and silently followed Derrick down the bleachers and into a deserted locker room. All sorts of messy thoughts went through his head, but they all narrowed down to one: *What am I doing alone with Derrick Cryder?!*

A year ago he would have known it meant instant pain, maybe even death. But ever since their little Christmas encounter Derrick had given up the bully business. Of course, he could be trying to make a comeback . . . and Nick could always be the first victim in his return engagement.

As they entered the room and the door swung shut, Derrick pointed forcefully to the nearest bench. Nick obeyed without speaking, without even thinking—well, except for wondering if his parents' health insurance would cover him for whatever was coming.

Derrick stepped toward him and growled, "What're you doin' hanging out with that loser?" He jabbed his finger back toward the door.

"Loser?" Nick croaked. "He . . . he's the most popular kid in school, Derrick!"

Derrick scowled harder.

Nick gave a swallow and continued. "And when I hang with him, I'm popular, too."

"Popular?!" Derrick shouted as he slammed his hand against a nearby locker. "I thought you knew what was important!"

"I do," Nick said, even more nervous over Derrick's outburst.

"You *did*," Derrick corrected. He shoved his face into Nick's. "When you stood up to me last Christmas—when you told me about God—then you knew something. But now . . . now I'm not sure you know anything, Martin."

He stepped back and looked down at Nicholas, who swallowed again . . . or at least tried. When you're going to die, sometimes it's hard to find anything to swallow.

But it wasn't Derrick's style to play destruction derby with people's faces anymore. Instead, he reached out and removed Nick's shades. "Be who you are, man," he said softly.

Nick looked up and blinked.

"These things don't fit you," Derrick said as he calmly folded up the glasses and stuck them into Nick's shirt pocket. Then, without a word, he turned and walked out the door.

Suddenly Nick was alone. All alone. He sat for a long moment trying to figure out what had just happened. Finally he stood up and started to adjust his hair. Then he saw it. His reflection in the mirror. And a sudden shock went through him. That wasn't him. It couldn't be. The black vest, black shirt, black pants . . . no way.

What *was* he doing? Who was he trying to be?

Derrick's voice rang loudly in his ears: "Be who you are, man." Nick slowly sank onto the bench.

EIGHT
Clear Vision

About the same time Nick and Rex were sneaking into the "Battle," the high schoolers across town were having a battle of their own—on the gridiron. Well, maybe *battle* isn't the right word; *massacre* is more like it. By halftime the visiting team had more points on their side of the scoreboard than most teams score in an entire season, while the hometown boys just couldn't seem to get rid of that big fat "0" on their side.

As the marching band stumbled out onto the field for halftime entertainment, Sarah and Jamie stood in the long line at the concession stand. It hadn't been Sarah's best week. She'd completely avoided Morgan; Tina had completely avoided her; and now she had to baby-sit her tagalong sister for the evening. Yes sir, on the scale of one to ten, this week was definitely somewhere in the minus column.

"Sarah." Jamie tugged at her shirt.

"Stop it," Sarah whispered out of the corner of her mouth. She smiled at a couple of passing kids, doing her best to pretend Jamie didn't exist. But if there was one thing Jamie was good at, it was making sure she wasn't ignored.

"Sarah—"

"You were supposed to keep three steps behind me!" Sarah scowled harshly. "What if somebody sees you're with me?"

"Let's just get the food," Jamie stated.

"You have any suggestions?" Sarah shot back. "I'm not Moses, and this crowd's not gonna part for us, no matter how much you whine."

"I wish we'd stayed at home. We're missing the *My Little Pony Meets Batman* special," she said, sulking. "Just 'cause you want to see Mr. Hunk in action."

"Morgan has nothing to do with me being here." The line moved up a person. "I told you," Sarah continued, "it's all over between us."

"Good thing," Jamie agreed. "I've never seen a team throw so many interruptions in my life."

"That's 'interceptions,'" Sarah corrected. "And since when do you know a football game from hopscotch?"

"I know a failed thirty-three green, right-split reverse when I see one."

Sarah stopped and gaped at her sister. She wasn't sure if Jamie knew what she was talking about or if she was just bluffing—it was hard to tell with Jamie. But Sarah did know one thing: The team had played an entire half, and Morgan hadn't gone in once.

Sarah and Jamie arrived at the counter and made their purchases as, out on the field, the marching band finished their halftime show. Everyone seemed grateful that the noise was over. There was something about all that drum pounding and out-of-tune playing that made people appreciate silence.

"So, where's your Morgan, anyway?" Jamie asked.

"I don't know." Sarah shrugged sadly. "It doesn't matter . . . not anymore."

A loud cheer erupted from the stands. Cheerleaders shouted, fans clapped, and, unfortunately, the band started to play as the teams raced back onto the field.

Armed with a corn dog and a couple of slices of rubbery pizza, Sarah and Jamie made their way back toward their seats. To one side was the grandstand, which was full of noisy and excited people. To the other side were the players on the sideline, yelling and pumping each other up for the second-half kickoff.

Sarah nibbled on her corn dog. Jamie ate her pizza, shoving it into her mouth like it was on a conveyor belt.

"Jamie!" Sarah scolded. "You're not supposed to eat pizza like a paper shredder! At least breathe once in a while!"

Jamie stopped long enough to catch her breath, then started in again. "Mit's meefa omma memamama mif mwam mwa." (Translation: "It's my pizza, and I can eat it any way I want.")

Suddenly there was a voice from the sideline. "Hey! Sarah!"

Sarah turned. "Morgan!" she gasped.

Yep, there he was—her ex-heartthrob . . . on crutches. "What happened?" she exclaimed.

"It looks worse than it is—just a twisted ankle. But it was enough to keep me outta the game." Then, spotting Jamie, he gave her a quick chuck under the chin. "Hey, how ya doin', short stuff?"

"Miff mumms mraumms," Jamie mumbled between bites.

The crowd started to roar—a sure sign that the kickoff was about to take place. Sarah and Morgan turned toward the field. Horns blared, cymbals crashed, and cheerleaders cartwheeled as the ball went sailing through the air and the Eastfield receiver moved under to catch it.

Cheers exploded as he caught the ball. Groans followed as he slipped and fell.

"Not going too well, is it?" Sarah asked meekly.

"Oh, there's still time." Morgan shrugged. "Swivel Hips Rick just has to settle down some. He'll do it. You'll see."

There was a moment of silence as Sarah and Morgan tried to figure out what to say next. Finally they both started, at the same time:

"Listen, I want to—"

"Morgan, I'm really—"

They both gave nervous laughs.

"Go ahead," Morgan offered.

"No, you," Sarah insisted, grateful that she wouldn't have to go first.

"Well . . ." Morgan took a deep breath. "I just want to say I know why you're avoiding me, and you're absolutely right!"

"I am?" Sarah asked, a little confused.

"Absolutely," he said with a nod. "I was a total jerk, making fun of the tennis team like that."

"But—"

Morgan held out his hand and continued. "I know you guys are really trying. Besides, what kind of idiot would make fun of people who are giving it their best shot?"

Sarah was caught off balance. Before she had a chance to answer, the bleachers suddenly erupted into cheers.

Fans leaped from their seats. Sarah and Morgan spun around to see what had happened.

"All right!" Morgan shouted, "First down! Way to go, Rick!" Then he turned back to Sarah. "Anyway, I just wanted to say I was sorry and I can understand why you don't want to be around me."

Sarah just stared, mouth agape. She wanted to say something, but at the moment nothing came to mind. Nothing at all.

Fortunately, Jamie always has something to say. "Close your mouth, Sarah, or you'll catch flies." (Good ol' Jamie.)

The barb brought Sarah back to reality. "I . . . uh . . ." She shook her head. "That's OK, Morgan. I'm the one who owes you an apology."

"Me?" Morgan asked.

"I had no business deceiving you—pretending to be something I'm not."

"You never deceiv—"

"Sure I did." Sarah took a gulp of air. It was true confessions time—something she'd been thinking about the whole week and something she finally had to get off her chest. "I should have told you right off the bat I was on the team, but I was too embarrassed. And because of that I not only lost you, I lost my best friend . . ." She forced out a little laugh. "Guess that makes me a loser all the way around."

"No," Morgan interrupted. "You're not a loser. Not to me."

Sarah looked up. There was no mistaking the sincerity in his eyes. Once again they were interrupted by the roar of the crowd. They looked out to the field just in time to see Swivel Hips Rick fire off a long, beautiful pass.

"All right!" Morgan cheered. "Way to go, Ricky!"

They continued to watch as the ball sailed long and high . . . right into the other team's arms for another perfect interception. The crowd groaned.

Morgan could only shake his head. "They're stomping us. I can't look—it's too embarrassing."

"I know the feeling," Sarah teased. "But don't worry, you'll get used to it."

Morgan looked up. For a moment she thought she'd gone too far. She wasn't sure if he was going to yell or laugh. Then she saw it: a grin forming on his lips. She broke into a broader smile.

Finally he spoke. "So when's your next match, Martin?"

"Why?"

"So I can be there and get more pointers on how to lose," he teased.

"You!" she said, giving him a poke in the ribs, and then another.

"Whoa!" he cried, almost losing his balance. She had to reach out and catch him or he and his crutches would have gone down for sure. And then somehow, some way, he had taken her hand . . . and he didn't let go.

Sarah beamed.

Jamie watched the whole thing. For once in her life she said nothing. She simply shook her head in disgust, wondering if there was any way to skip being a teenager.

Nick was suffering big-time teen pangs himself. He was leaning against the gym wall, watching everyone having fun. For some reason he felt like he was barely there. He felt like some sort of space alien watching while everyone else laughed and had a great time.

Mrs. Pryce was back at the microphone. "All right . . . are you groovy guys and gals hip to start the Big Battle?"

Hoots and cheers answered her question.

"OK, then, it's my pleasure to introduce two former Eastfield students who, twenty-five years ago tonight, started our very first Battle of the Bands."

Nick wiped the sweat from his forehead. Here it came. He had no doubt that it would be the most embarrassing moment of his life. His only question was, would the humiliation come quickly and mercifully, or would it be dragged out through the entire dance?

Mrs. Pryce continued, "Those two very special people went on to become husband and wife, and they're back with us to host tonight's battle. Please put your hands together for David and Elizabeth Martin."

Applause filled the gym as Mom and Dad stepped up to the microphone. Nick looked surprised. He thought the kids would fall down laughing—not applaud. He looked around, confused. It—it was almost like they . . . *liked* his dad!

Dad took the microphone as the applause began to fade. "Thank you all very much." He grinned. "You know, Mrs. Pryce, twenty-five years hasn't changed this place much." He gestured toward the wall. "The drinking fountain still doesn't work."

It was a corny joke, but everyone laughed along with it. Everyone but Nick. He still wasn't sure what to do.

Dad continued. "It's a great honor for Elizabeth and me

217

to be here tonight. In a few moments, we're gonna introduce some of the most talented young musicians in all of Eastfield. There will be four bands, each doing a set of fifteen minutes." Applause again filled the room along with some scattered cheers and yells.

"But before we do that . . ." Dad lifted his hand to quiet them. "As one Eastfield Eagle to another, I'd like to offer each of you a special challenge."

The noise died down. Everyone began to listen.

"You know, this is one of the most important times of your life. A lot of what's going to happen to you later on is going to start right here in junior high." He paused a moment to let the point sink in. "So get a good start," he continued. "Believe in yourself, in your family . . . and in friends who really care about you."

The words hit Nick dead center. He knew Dad hadn't planned it that way, but that didn't stop the words from hitting their mark.

"And above all, understand who you are and what you believe in, here," Dad said, touching his heart, "inside. Be yourself. Be the person God made you to be."

Nick felt his face getting a little hot. He looked around again, afraid of what he would see. But his schoolmates were quiet, and all eyes were fixed on Dad. The kids could tell the man meant what he was saying. They knew he believed it, and at least for that moment they believed it, too.

Come to think of it . . . so did Nick.

"And now," Dad said, suddenly lightening up, "I'll step aside and let the Battle begin!"

The audience cheered. Yelps and catcalls rattled the raf-

218

ters as Dad made the first introduction: "Starting with the moldy oldie that opened the first battle . . . take it away, The Armadillos!"

But before the audience could break into applause Principal Pryce suddenly reappeared. In her hand was a saxophone.

"Hold on a second, David. You're gonna either love me or hate me for this," she shoved the saxophone into his hands, "but would you do us the honor of blowing a little riff on this first song, just like you did twenty-five years ago?"

Again the audience broke into loud cheers as the curtain opened behind them. There was the band, tuned up and ready to play. For a second Dad protested, but the audience cheered him on until, reluctantly, he clipped the horn to its neck strap and sighed. "Whew . . ." was all he said, but it brought another wave of applause.

He looked back to the band. They were waiting.

Nick quietly bit his lip.

"Well," Dad sighed again, "here goes nothing. You guys ready?"

The players in the band nodded. The drummer clicked off the opening beats with his sticks, and the music began. Dad took a deep breath, put the saxophone to his lips, and started the opening bars. The first few notes were a little weak and self-conscious, but soon Dad was rocking like a pro.

The audience was right with him, cheering and clapping.

Nick couldn't believe his ears—or his heart. He was

actually proud of his dad. And the guy wasn't even trying to be anything . . . he was just Dad.

Nicholas glanced over at Mom. She was watching "her man" rip off the tune. She had her hands together like they had frozen in mid-clap, and you could tell from her smile why they were married, why they were such good friends, and why they were such a happy family.

Friends . . . family, Nick thought. *What have I done to them . . . to all of them?*

His eyes moved from Mom to the snack table where Philip, Renee, and Jordan were drinking punch. They were smiling, laughing, and having a great time. But how could they, the "uncool," be so happy?

What was more, if you could be happy without being cool, what was the point of working so hard to be cool? Come to think of it, how happy had he been since he moved into the world of "ultracool"? Oh sure, people had finally begun to notice him. But was he happy?

Hyperstressed? Maybe.

Guilty? Absolutely.

But happy? No way.

Nick watched Philip. He remembered the eager look on his face when he'd told Nick about the computer show. Then there was the memory of happy-go-lucky Jordan tossing his football into the air. The guy was always so accepting, always so happy.

Nicholas glanced over at Rex and his clones. They looked anything but happy. After all, it was against the "cool code" to enjoy anything. Feelings weren't cool, caring wasn't cool, friends weren't cool, love wasn't cool.

He remembered how nervous he'd been when Rex was

over for dinner and they'd held hands. He thought about all the love around the table—love that his family felt toward each other and toward the Lord. Definitely "uncool," but definitely good. Very, very good.

He looked back to his dad, still rocking away on the sax, then to his mom laughing and clapping . . . and he groaned inwardly. The image of their expressions when he told them he wasn't going with them to the Battle of the Bands floated in his mind. He'd hurt them—a lot.

And finally, there was McGee, his longest and best friend. . . . Nick frowned, a sick feeling in his gut.

That was it. Nick knew what he had to do. It wouldn't be easy. And it definitely wouldn't be "cool." But he was going to do it.

Nicholas turned and started toward Rex and the gang.

NINE
Wrapping Up

As Dad's saxophone wailed, Nick's mind raced.

How had he gotten himself into such a mess? More important, how was he going to get himself out? However he did it, there was no way he could do it and still look cool. But then, looking cool wasn't such a big deal. Doing the right thing—that was the ticket. And as much as Nick hated to admit it, he knew what that right thing was.

He continued toward Rex, slowly at first. With any luck maybe there'd be a giant earthquake before he arrived. Or a tornado. Shoot, right now he'd settle for a good old-fashioned flash flood. But there was nothing. Just the hooting and hollering of the crowd as Dad continued his sax solo . . . and Nicholas started up the bleachers.

"Hey, dude," Rex shouted as he approached. "Your dad blows a pretty mean 'phone for a fossil." He laughed, giving the cue to Babs and Jessica to follow along. They giggled.

"Yeah," Nick agreed, turning back to look at his dad. "He is pretty good, isn't he?"

Rex continued. "The three of us were thinking about sneaking into the flicks later tonight. What do you say?"

Nicholas turned back to Rex. He had wanted to be like this guy for weeks. He'd wanted people to admire him. He'd wanted girls dangling from his arms. He'd wanted people eating up his every word. But now . . .

Now the price was too high. It wasn't worth forgetting who he was to be someone he wasn't. Well, it was now or never. Nicholas took a deep breath. "Look, Rex, uh . . . thanks for the invite—and for letting me hang out with you—but, uh, I . . . think I've had enough."

There, he'd done it. He'd said no to Rex and yes to who he was. He stood there a second. It was all over, just like that. Finally he started to turn away, but stopped. Something else had to be done. Something to seal the deal, to make sure there was no turning back.

"Oh, and one more thing," Nick said as he turned to Rex. He reached into his pocket and pulled out his sunglasses. "Here. I don't see too well with these on."

He handed them to Rex.

For a moment the guy looked kinda confused. But Nick knew he'd eventually figure it out. So he simply turned and walked back down the bleachers.

Rex watched in astonishment. The look on his face told the whole story. It was clear that nobody had ever turned his back on him—not the great Rexster! Who did this punk think he was, anyway? After all, he'd taken the geek in, shown him the ropes, taught him what it was to be cool . . . given him a chance to be somebody. And now he just walks away?

Rex wanted to say something—he wanted to shout at Nick, tell him what a loser he was, but shouting wasn't cool. Shouting meant you cared. And Rex was too cool to care. Instead, he shut down his emotions and shifted into ultracool. He chuckled to the girls as he shoved the shades into his pocket. "Once a loser, always a loser," he said with a smirk. Babs and Jessica giggled right on cue. Just like always.

Meanwhile, Derrick had seen the whole thing from across the gym. "Way to go, Martin." He smiled to himself. "Way to go."

Nick continued moving through the crowd. It was like he was waking up from a dream. Everything was a blur—the lights, the kids, even the music was a mishmash of sounds. Except for the sax. He stopped beside one of the cardboard decorations on the wall, a Corvette cutout, to watch his dad. Nick grinned. Maybe it wouldn't be so bad to be like him when he grew up. Without, of course, the hair and bell-bottoms.

He turned to look around—and spotted them.

Renee, Philip, and Jordan were clustered together across the room. Nick swallowed hard. They were his friends. At least, they used to be. He'd betrayed them. No question. If they refused to talk to him for the rest of his life, he couldn't blame them.

He turned and started to walk away. He'd already been through one emotional roller coaster. He didn't need another "Maalox moment."

But he'd only taken a few steps before he stopped. With a sigh, he knew he couldn't just walk away. He had to set things right, even if it meant total rejection.

He turned, took a deep breath, and started forward.

They didn't see him coming, not until he reached out and tapped Renee on the shoulder. "Hey, dudes," he said

with a smile. Oops! Wrong intro. Try again. "I mean . . .
hi, guys. Mind if I hang with you?"

Renee looked up. It was hard to read what she was
thinking. Without a word she turned to Jordan. Jordan
hesitated, then turned to Philip. All three looked at each
other. It seemed to take forever for them to make up their
minds. Finally, in perfect three-part unison, they shook
their heads and said "Nahhhhhhh"—and turned their
backs on him.

Nicholas's heart sank. He'd heard of rejection, but this
gave the word a whole new meaning. "Guys?" he pleaded
to their backs.

They didn't budge. Not for a whole millisecond. Then
they couldn't hold it in any longer. They started giggling
. . . first a little, then a lot. Finally they turned back to
Nicholas, laughing. Renee tousled his hair, Jordan poked
his stomach, and Philip gave him a punch on the arm.
Nick knew they each, in their own ways, were saying,
"We're glad you're back . . . but don't you ever, ever do
that to us again!"

He broke into a grin. He wanted to say something powerful, something profound, something that would show
the depths of his feelings. But all that came out was a thick
kind of "I'm sorry," followed by an embarrassed shrug.

His friends understood perfectly.

"We wondered when you were gonna shrug off those
ice cubes," Jordan said with a smirk.

Pointing at his clothes, Renee quipped, "We thought
they'd shrink-wrapped your brain in black leather."

"OK, OK," Nick laughed. "All I can do is plead tempo-
rary insanity."

226

Everyone laughed in agreement. This was easier than Nick had imagined. They'd forgiven him almost instantly. But maybe that's one of the main ingredients of "uncoolness" . . . loving enough to forgive.

Suddenly the room exploded in applause! Dad had just ended his number with a big flourish, and the crowd went wild! Dad beamed. Not only did he manage to impress the crowd, he looked a little impressed himself. And then, at last, he caught Nicholas's eye.

But instead of shrinking or ducking his head, Nick actually raised his arm and gave him a thumbs-up. Dad turned and looked behind himself to see who his son was motioning to, but there was no one in back of him. He turned to Nick, giving him the ol' "Who? Me?" gesture.

Nick laughed.

Dad grinned and stepped off the stage. Immediately he was joined by Mom as he moved through the congratulating crowd—but he barely slowed down. He was determined to reach his son.

When his parents finally arrived, Nick struggled for the right words, but nothing came. That was OK; no words were necessary. Somehow Dad already knew. He smiled and gave Nicholas a brief hug—a very brief hug (after all, they were still surrounded by junior highers). But it made no difference to Nick. For the first time in a long while, he didn't care about being embarrassed.

But it wasn't entirely over—not just yet . . .

When the boy blunder and Pops finished their little huggy-huggy scene, I figured it was time to make my reappearance. After all, Nicky boy had definitely learned his lesson. It was time for me to stop giving him the silent treatment and come out of hiding. (The fact that he started to imagine me again didn't hurt, either.)

"You know, kid," I said as I hopped up on his foot, "I kinda missed ya."

He looked down and yelped, "McGee! You're back!"

"Not only my back," I quipped as I turned around, "but also my fabulous front and two sensational sides."

Nick gave me one of his world-famous "McGee-I-love-you-but-knock-it-off-with-the-stupid-jokes" looks.

Quicker than you can say, "It looks like we're coming to the end of this little tale," I hopped off his shoe and went over to my souped-up, cherry red McGeemobile. Throwing on my goggles and scarf, I crossed over and opened the hood. "It took a while, but I'm glad you finally found out what's cool."

"You're right," Nick agreed. "Being who you are, that's what's really cool."

"No, no, no," I corrected. "It's cars. Cars are what's cool!"

I ducked my head (and everything else except for my toes) under the hood. "Three-eighty-five, dual cams, overdrive—it doesn't get much cooler than this."

"McGee," the kid started to protest.

"Watch this!" I shouted as I slammed down the hood and hopped behind the wheel.

"What are you doing?" Nick asked in obvious jealousy.

"Peelin' rubber," I said with a grin as I stepped on the gas. "WHOOOAAA . . . NELLIE!"

I took off and left a skid mark the size of the national debt on the floor. I never knew such power. I never knew such speed. I never learned how to drive. . . .

"L O O K O U T ! ! !"

It was demolition derby time.

VVVAAAROOOOOOOOOOOOOM!

Everywhere I turned there were shoes . . . hundreds of dancing shoes. I swerved back and forth and back and forth. And then, when I got tired of that, I started swerving forth and back and forth and back.

It did no good. I couldn't keep this up forever. It was time to do what I did best: time to assert my genuinely great genius, to motivate my manly machoness, to scream my head off for help.

"NICHOLAS!"

But that didn't do any good, either. Ol' Nicky was too busy pointing and laughing. And then, finally, it happened. There were no more shoes. Ah, what luck, what fortune, what FEAR!!

"Somebody . . . move that stage!!"

There it was, dead ahead (a rather unfortunate choice of words, but have you ever heard of something being "live ahead?" I didn't think so). In any case, I was heading straight toward the stage. Not a bad place for someone with my great talents, but at the moment I had no more songs or jokes. I'd left all my song-and-dance stuff back in chapter 5.

But not to worry your pretty little heads, dear reader. I'll get out of this. I always do. Besides, Book Twelve is just around the corner, and you wouldn't dream of reading a book with just the title "And Me!" on the cover. Right?

I mean you'd want another name in the front. Right? Something that starts with "Mc" . . . and maybe ends in a couple of es . . . with a big G stuck in the middle?

Right?

Ahem, I said, "Right?"

OK. Fine. If you want to be that way about it, you'll just have to excuse me. I have a little more screaming to do.

"NICHOLAS!! GET ME OUT OF HERE! N I C H O -
L A S ! ! ! ! !"